RAMILLIES

By the same author

The Caretaker Wife
Quicksilver Lady

RAMILLIES

Barbara Whitehead

ST. MARTIN'S PRESS NEW YORK

Library of Congress Cataloging in Publication Data

Whitehead, Barbara.
Ramillies.

I. Title.
PR6073.H543R3 1984 823'.914 83-21173
ISBN 0-312-66344-7

First published in Great Britain in 1983 by Methuen London Ltd

First U.S. Edition

10 9 8 7 6 5 4 3 2 1

This book is lovingly dedicated to my uncle,
Herbert Stanley Oliver.

The house in this story, Ramillies, is based, with permission, on Castle Howard in Yorkshire. Every visitor to that house walks past the altar from the Temple of the Oracle at Delphi, which was presented to the fifth Earl of Carlisle by Sir William Hamilton. This altar was the inspiration for part of the story. Many of the visitors to the gardens go up to the Temple of the Four Winds, which was the original of the Temple of Fortune in this book. This little building has for a long time been my favourite piece of English architecture.

I am grateful to Castle Howard, York, for help with the locations for this work, and also to Mrs Joan Field, for her verse for the Oracle. The invocation to Apollo is taken from lines by William Mason, 1724–1797.

Contents

CHAPTER ONE

The Mouse

The Prince Regent, that vast, charming, sentimental, disgusting prince, had at last succeeded to his inheritance, had become George the Fourth, and was daily in fear that his Queen would arrive in England. Caroline of Brunswick-Wolfenbüttel was on a triumphant progress across Europe towards England and nothing anyone could say would stop her. It provided a good talking point in the tranquil countryside of eighteen twenty, where life was otherwise so uneventful that even a very little mouse could assume importance.

The year had just edged its way into June. In the morning-room of Langbar Hall, Bella Langbar and her cousin Laetitia, Countess of Elmet, were alone, when Laetitia saw the mouse. 'Oh!' she cried out, startled, and Bella turned and saw it too. The cat was crouching under the table, right up against the painted wainscot and the mouse – such a little mouse – was within six inches of its nose.

In an instant Laetitia had taken in everything about the mouse. The humped, defiant body in its ruffled grey fur; the tiny claws on minute, pinkish feet; the bravery, as it faced the cat.

'Can't we save it?' she said.

'I wish Soot wouldn't bring mice in here when he catches them,' complained Bella. 'Why can't he eat them outside?'

'He hasn't caught this one. I mean, he must have caught it to bring it in, but it looks unhurt. Bella, it is only little. Don't you think we could save it?'

'Save it for what?' asked Bella with some contempt. 'So that it can run away and breed more mice?'

'We could let it go in the garden, or the gardener would kill it quickly.'

'The cat will kill it quickly enough,' replied Bella with indifference and turned away, going to her seat between the window and the fire.

Although it was June, the weather was cold and damp and the large, airy room gained an extra touch of luxury from the burning logs on their bed of glowing embers, with the dance of transparent flames above them. Outside, the park of Langbar Hall lay moistly green and undulating, its groups of trees heavy with their summer leaves. They had soaked up water till they could hold no more. Now they were like great emerald sponges, floating on a floodtide of green.

Both the young women were in light summer gowns, with muslin sleeves over their arms and muslin up to the lace ruffles round their throats. Bella was more solidly built than her slender cousin, and dark, whereas Laetitia was charmingly fair. Bella now picked up a hank of black silk and separated out a strand, then threaded the needle which had been left sticking into the border of her embroidery. The stretched linen on the frame bore a faint design of a weeping willow drooping over an urn, and she prepared to concentrate on her stitches.

'Would you like to read to me?' she asked.

Laetitia was still standing in the centre of the room, her deep blue eyes tragic, watching the scene under the table. If she interfered, Soot would undoubtedly scratch her, and Bella was probably right. At last she turned and walked over towards her cousin and as though her going had released some spell the mouse made a dash, ran to a low chest and disappeared under it a blink of time before the cat reached it. Biting her rosy underlip, Laetitia watched the foiled cat, which crouched on the shining boards with its nose pressed to the floor, whiskers twitching, tail slowly moving from side to side, and all its life concentrated in its golden eyes.

'Fetch a book and read to me,' asked Bella again.

'Yes . . . yes . . . what would you like?'

'Anything. Mama will be back soon and you know how she hates to see us idle. And I like to hear you read.'

Laetitia acknowledged the truth of this. Ten years of living with her Aunt had not made the task any easier. When Laetitia had first come to Langbar Hall, an unhappy, lonely orphan, her Aunt had adopted a tone towards her which was meant to be bracing. This would have suited her own children, who had inherited her thick-skinned qualities, but it had meant misery to the shy, sensitive Laetitia.

To be idle was a sin at Langbar Hall and it would be best if they were both doing something when Lady Langbar came in. There would soon be other disturbances to their peace. Bella's two younger sisters would be coming from their lessons in the schoolroom and all would be noise and confusion. None of the quiet harmony Laetitia craved was to be found in Langbar Hall.

She slipped out of the room and to the dark library, returning in a few minutes with a novel in her hand.

The cat, growing impatient, was growling in its throat and reaching under the chest with one paw.

'He hasn't still got that mouse there, has he?' asked Laetitia.

Bella stuck her needle into her work and went over to the chest.

'Oh, no, Bella! Let it escape, poor little thing!'

'Do you think that is kind? Do you think it is better to let it die down a hole, in pain and slowly, or is it kinder to let Soot kill it? Let us make an end!'

'Don't, Bella!' Laetitia ran over to the chest and put her hands on it to hold it firm. Bella had seen her gentle cousin over-ruled too often to heed her. With a heave she moved the chest to one side. For an instant it was a frozen picture. The mouse was sitting in the very centre of the space, its paws together in front of its chest, its ears alert. Then the picture was fractured by movement as the cat pounced and threw into the air the ball of grey fur. It flew past Laetitia and she gasped, feeling the air full of tormented creatures. After a hurly-burly of movement cat and mouse ended together in a different corner, quite empty of furniture, with nothing but the angle of walls and floor to complicate matters.

The door opened and Lady Langbar entered, filling the room at once by her presence. With a comprehensive glance she took in the whole: her golden-haired niece, flushed and in some disorder, returning to her chair and hastily picking up the book which had been dropped beside it; her own daughter with compressed lips, taking the needle out again from its resting place in the linen.

'What is going on?' she asked.

'Nothing, Mama. Soot has a mouse and Laetitia wanted to save it and let it go in the garden.'

'It is such a little mouse,' Laetitia tried to excuse herself.

'Little mice, my dear,' said Lady Langbar magisterially, 'grow into big mice. They are vermin and must be kept down. Bella was right and I'm afraid you were wrong. We wish Soot to catch them, that is his work in life. You must not discourage him. Mice cause damage and create an unpleasant smell.'

Laetitia opened the book in her hands and looked down at it through a mist of tears. She wondered what was her own work in life, for she was determined to go on resisting Lady Langbar's plans for her. Was she as useful as the cat? Could she bear to continue living at Langbar Hall where nothing she did or said was right and where her work in life was reading to Bella, or riding, or walking in the park?

'Do not let me interrupt the reading,' said her Aunt. Laetitia pulled herself together. 'I thought you might like to hear this one again,' she said to Bella in her gentle voice. 'It is two years since I read it to you.'

'What is it?' broke in her Aunt, leaning forward and examining the book. 'Oh yes. *Pride and Prejudice*, I see. A pretty kind of story. The heroine, I remember, marries a man of consequence, stands out for him against a less advantageous match. You must look out for yourself, my dear, in marriage. Your mother did very well, catching the Earl of Elmet. You must take care to bestow yourself suitably. Bella's choice pleases me very much.'

'Yes, Aunt.'

'I often tell you this, I know, Letty – it is of such importance. You must make a suitable alliance, child.'

'Yes, Aunt.'

Bella's needle flashed in the sunlight.

'You have the looks. It is a pity you have so little spirit. You must not hang back behind Bella when I take you out. Your rank entitles you to be first in almost any assembly. The Special Remainder enabling your father's title and estates to pass through the female line gave you a consequence which very few women have. I sometimes wonder if you realize that. I would like to see a little pride, my dear, in you. A little stateliness and presence.'

'Yes, Aunt.'

In the corner the mouse made another run for it, was fielded and batted back into the angle of the walls, and then curled up into a hopeless grey ball one inch across.

Laetitia began to read. '"It is a fact universally acknowledged, that a single man in possession of a good fortune, must be in want of a wife . . ."'

She was interrupted by the entrance of a footman with a letter on a silver salver. Lady Langbar took the letter, waved her fingers in dismissal to the footman and broke the seal. Her niece's reading went on in the background until her own more strident tones over-rode Laetitia's as though they had never existed.

'Here is a pretty kettle of fish!'

Bella looked up, but her parent's expression was unreadable.

'What is it, Mama? Can you tell us?'

'There can be no secret of it. The letter is from your father. He has decided to stay the night with the Greys, and will not be back until tomorrow morning. He thought I would want to hear the news at once that the Earl of the Ainsty is dead.'

'The Earl of the Ainsty!'

'Dead!'

'But we saw him only last week and he was in health!'

'He has only been Earl for a twelvemonth!'

'You mean the ninth Earl, I collect, Mama?'

'Yes, I mean the ninth Earl, who succeeded last year – who did you think I meant? He has been killed in an accident out riding.'

'How? What a dreadful thing!'

'His horse fell at a fence and rolled on him. They took him up at once – he was seen by men working in the fields – and he was alive then, your father says. By the time they had carried him to the nearest house and fetched the apothecary from Malton, he was dead.'

There was silence in the morning-room until Bella said, 'I wonder what will happen now, to Ramillies?'

'What a waste.' Lady Langbar did not heed her daughter. 'Young, rich and unmarried.' She stroked the cat, which had jumped up on to her lap. 'It was as your book says, Letty, a single man in possession of a good fortune and in want of a wife. What a pity you would not have him! There would have been time to give birth to an heir and you would now have been in a most advantageous position – there would just have been time – you would have been left regent of Ramillies.'

At this, Laetitia looked down at her book with burning cheeks. There was to be hope in her life then, after all. The news in this letter had removed the threats and hinted pressures which had been hanging over her. Then, too, while her Aunt and cousin had been preoccupied, she had noticed that the mouse had also escaped. It had run again, vanished, and the cat, considering it lost, had given up the pursuit. And now that the Earl of the Ainsty had died, she too had escaped, and could, if she were circumspect, live unobtrusively a little longer . . .

'But who will inherit Ramillies?' persisted Bella.

Miss Jane Austen might equally well have written that a man in possession of a good wife must be in want of a fortune. This was a truth which had been painfully discovered some years earlier, by Ensign Akeham. He had wooed and married the best wife in the world and his family had acknowledged the match by cutting him off without a penny.

As his Mollie was the orphan daughter of a poor clergyman, there was no help from that quarter either. When he met her, she was spending the summer with a maiden aunt near Brighton, and he was in the militia camp established there in seventeen ninety-three.

If Ensign Akeham had only known it, that was the way of the world. If he had pleased his family by marrying any of the young ladies they had in mind for him, with fortunes of their own, he would have been rewarded by receiving his parents' entire approval and a continuing, nay, an increasing allowance. He might well have ended as a major. As it was, the young couple were compelled to exist on his meagre pay; and very happy indeed they were on it.

But a few years after their marriage, Ensign Akeham was foolishly and heroically killed in a skirmish against the French, leaving his Mollie with a little curly-haired son and no provision at all for their future livelihood.

She made her way back to England and to the village where she had lived as a girl. Her father had held the living there and his brother, her uncle, was now the incumbent. Part of his demesne was a small cottage opening straight on to the village green, and this he allowed Mollie to occupy rent free. There, scraping a living on what little she had received from the army and a minute legacy she had inherited from the aunt at Brighton, she had brought up and educated her son as best she could.

Harry Akeham's cradle had been rocked by gunfire and until they went to live in the cottage in Cherry Wigston he had known no settled home, for they had moved constantly from one set of married quarters to another. He was a happy, contented child and his chatter had cheered his mother on their journey to her home village. Once there, his delight in the countryside of her own childhood had helped her to come to terms with her widowed life. Quite soon she began to think of him as a companion, because he was always so interested in all that she did and that went on around them. He was not the kind of boy who shouts and tears his clothes. Rather, he was the neat-handed kind who are often to be found flying a home-made kite on the common, brambling along the hedges, or carving something immensely useful out of an odd piece of wood. When he was about eight he began to get up early and light the fire for her, and share in the care of the poultry.

In the nearby market town there was an ancient Free Grammar School, and there Harry did passably well. By the time he was fourteen and nearing the end of his education, Nelson had led the navy to victory at Trafalgar, but Napoleon had been invincible on land. Britain and France were locked in war in the Peninsula.

Most of the sons of the local gentry went to the Grammar School, and were educated hugger-mugger with the sons of tradesmen and other lesser lights. It was not until the end of their schooldays that Harry Akeham realized that he himself was neither fish, flesh, fowl nor good red herring.

His friends who were the sons of gentlemen were preparing for Oxford or Cambridge. His friends who were the sons of tradesmen were taking up apprenticeships. But what was Harry himself to do? If he could have chosen, he thought that an apprenticeship to an attorney or a surgeon-apothecary might have suited him very well. His mother would have liked him to go into the church. He might have been able to do that, by winning one of the few scholarships which were available. He would then have had to eke out an existence as a poor scholar and become an even poorer curate, with little chance of preferment. But he had no inclination for the church and the fees demanded for apprenticeships were out of reach.

So Harry made up his mind and tried to look cheerful about it because he did not want to upset his mother. He accepted the offer of his old schoolmaster and stayed on at the Grammar School as an assistant. It was not well paid and had no prospects, but there were compensations. He could go on living at home and keeping his mother company, and Harry was by nature considerate and chivalrous and her welfare was important to him. They were used, after all, to poverty.

He remained for some years at this post. His old headmaster died and the new man began to make his life a misery. Then a rich tradesman in the town, who needed a tutor for his invalid son, made him a good offer, which Harry accepted. He still lived at home and walked in to his work every morning. He liked his pupil and his work was much lighter than at the school. The larger salary meant that Mollie could begin to save, for they lived as frugally as ever.

All this time their lives had been quiet and uneventful, for great events did not come to Cherry Wigston. They heard of what was happening in the outside world, of Wellington's conquest of Napoleon at Waterloo, of the exile of the defeated despot to St Helena and then to Elba. Then the country faced up to the aftermath of war. This did affect them, for it affected everybody. People muttered about the victors in the late war being worse off than the vanquished, which is often the way of wars.

Things were adjusting themselves a little by this particular wet and sodden June. They heard that the Prince Regent, old by now himself, was at last King in name as well as fact. They heard how the new manufacturing towns were growing as power was applied to their industries. Cherry Wigston was unchanged; as it had been for time out of mind and as it would be, for ever.

It might have seemed to outsiders that Harry Akeham's fate was nothing out of the ordinary. They might even have pitied him a little. Yet he was, on this certain day in mid-June, a happy man. He had good health, a good appetite, a good temper, and if he had ever thought about it, he would have decided that no one in the wide world could be happier.

The whole drowsy village seemed to be at peace. There was only one disgruntled creature in Cherry Wigston, the old heron who usually fished the river there, and who considered that the village belonged to him.

The heron was a distinguished presence, a venerable presence. He was a personage who considered himself affronted, as he flew on slowly-moving grey wings up over the village and circled widely in the air, legs trailing, like some revived archaeopteryx, wise grey head held at an indignant angle, furious eye regarding the pleasant spread of countryside below him.

Cherry Wigston was only a short way outside the market town. The coach road ran through the village and it was quite familiar to travellers as a brief glimpse of a pretty duck-pond and a few cottages scattered round a village green. They might even notice a river hardly larger than a stream, curving under the bridge as they dashed across it. There was only an ale-house in Cherry Wigston, no inn, as none of the coaches ever stopped. It was too close to the town for fresh horses to be needed, or refreshments. It was only an incident on a journey for all except those who lived there.

The indignant heron, describing his wide circle in the sky over the village, could see a coach labouring up the hill on the approach road. The June rains had made the road wetter than usual in summer. He circled over the vicarage and there was the vicar's daughter, Harry's half-cousin, Mary, feeding her doves. The heron viewed her with a jaundiced eye. As he was not a grain eater she was no good to him.

Harry had once, when he was fourteen and did not know what direction his life was to take, fancied himself in love with the nineteen-year-old Mary. She had laughed at him and said that she would not want to live in a cottage and feed hens when she could live in a vicarage and feed doves, and later he had forgotten his adolescent partiality. He had made up his mind that for him it must always be no fortune therefore no wife. Harry and Mary were friends as well as cousins, and later that day Mary was half expecting Harry and his mother round to drink tea. They were quite at leisure to do so for Harry was on holiday. His employer had taken his family to Scarborough for a fortnight and given Harry leave to stay at home.

The great bird flew on over the cottage on the green where Harry lived with his mother and saw Widow Akeham, as people called poor pretty Mollie, going out into her garden at the back of the cottage to weed the flowers and collect the eggs. She was pretty Mollie still, in her plain print gown and simple cap, though it was now a comfortable, spreading kind of prettiness. The heron did not miss his slow wing-beat for her.

He saw from his aerial viewpoint that the coach had stopped, against all custom. Two passengers got down from it. Never had he seen a coach stop in Cherry Wigston. He had been disturbed at his fishing, and now the coach had stopped!

The bird settled on the top of a tall tree and curled one leg under his feathers, looking down at the river where it curved deep and soft through the meadows. There was his fishing pool where he had gone an hour earlier in the hope of catching his dinner, and there, sitting with their legs in the water, were Harry Akeham and Billy, the small boy from the ale-house.

Harry had a liking for herons and would gladly have joined him quietly and hoped to share the water with him. But the presence of Billy was enough to frighten every fish for miles. At the sound of him crashing through the still-wet grass, and the sight of him rushing and tumbling in his excitement like an untrained puppy, the venerable heron had risen from the water and, with undignified haste, scrambled up anyhow into the air and trailed off wetly into the sky.

As the coach drove off and left them, the two passengers who had climbed down from it to the green at Cherry Wigston stood uncertainly and looked about them, wondering what to do next. The place appeared deserted. But the wife of the owner of the ale-house had noticed them through the window and had called her husband up from the cellar. He came out and crossed over to them to ask what they wanted and if he could be of any assistance.

The strangers were a great contrast one to the other. One was a big, dark man who spoke very little, and the other was an odd, wizened, bit of a man, who did all the talking. They were dressed in a town fashion.

'My good man, I believe this is Cherry Wigston,' began the older, smarter man. The ale-house keeper agreed that it was. 'We are in search of a young gentleman, Mr Henry Akeham. We believe he lives here.'

The ale-house keeper rubbed his chin. 'There's Akehams in the village, yes, sir. There's Widow Akeham, vicar's niece, and her lad, Harry. I don't know of any gentleman called Mr Henry Akeham.'

'How old is this lad you spoke of, called Harry?'

'Bless me,' looking round for his wife, who had come out into the fresh air to wash the small winking panes of their front window. 'Hannah, how old is Widow Akeham's Harry?'

'He'll be twenty-six come Michaelmas,' answered the ale-wife. Then she took advantage of the query to put down her pail of soap-suds and join the group, standing at her ease and listening.

'What does he do for a living?' asked the bulky dark man, rousing in the ale-house keeper suspicion and hostility.

'Begging your pardon, sir, but you have no right to come here and ask questions like that. How folks get their livings is their own affair.'

'Yes, yes,' broke in the little man with a pacifying wave of the hand. 'We have very good news for the man we seek. We only ask questions to discover if your Harry Akeham is the Mr Henry Akeham we are looking for.'

'Hannah,' asked her husband doubtfully, 'was young Harry christened Henry?'

'Of course he was, you daft-head,' said the wifely Hannah. 'Just same as you were christened William and so was our Billy.'

'Was his mother Miss Verity before her marriage?' pressed the little man.

'She's niece to parson and he's Mr Verity,' was the cautious agreement.

'You'd best talk to them yourself,' put in Hannah. 'Widow Akeham will be at home.'

'Our business is really with Mr Henry Akeham.'

'Now, he's down at the river with our Billy. You'd best fetch him, Will. Would you step inside, gentlemen, and sit down? You'd welcome a glass of ale, I daresay?'

For the lack of something better to do for the next few minutes and as the sky in its muffling of grey clouds held out the possibility of rain, the two strangers gave in to Hannah and entered the ale-house to sit uncomfortably in the front room with the cat. They were watched over by the baby, who waved his rattle at them from his cradle in the corner.

Harry could not have said quite why he was spending only his second morning at home on holiday from teaching his invalid pupil in instructing young Billy on the art of fishing. It might have been that after his pupil's pale cheeks and languid eyes there was a charm in Billy's robust health, rosy cheeks, general grubbiness and the bouncing way he dashed at life. Or it might have been that down by the river he was re-living his memories of being a carefree boy himself, sitting for hours at a time on the river bank with a bent pin and a length of twine on a willow rod.

It is certain that at the moment when Will Shorthose was sent blundering down to the river to fetch him, Harry, with his feet in the water and Billy clutching the rod beside him, would not have changed places with a king. 'Oh, Lord, Will,' he remonstrated, 'whoever would be wanting me?'

There was a doubtful expression on Will's honest face as he looked at Harry's bare feet as Harry pulled himself up out of the water on to the bank. 'They asked for Mr Henry Akeham,' he said.

'Oh!' Harry shook his head. He picked up his hand-knitted stockings and stout leather shoes. 'I suppose I'd better come. Are you all right there, young Billy? Don't fall in, or your mother will have something to say to me.'

Billy did not bother to answer him as he had his tongue protruding between his teeth and his attention wholly on the river. This last remark, though, had worried his father.

'You'd best come too, our Billy. You can fish in the duck pond where we can see you,' he said, hauling his protesting son out of the water.

At least one being in the village was pleased by the arrival of the strangers. The heron, after a few minutes spent waiting to be sure that Harry and Billy had really gone, flew down again to the river, settled in his favourite spot, and, hunched and motionless, forgot everything else in his concentration on the rippling stream eddying round his spindly legs and on, past him, past the village. Where the stream ultimately journeyed, the heron did not care.

The two strangers were city lawyers. They were feeling tired and irritated as they sat in the humble ale-house of Cherry Wigston and sipped at their tankards of home-brew. They had spent some time in tracking down the man they were to interview and hoped that their efforts would be amply rewarded in the future, yet they did not expect to like him. Brought up in this place, with only rural company and occupations, he would be, they assumed, a country bumpkin and they expected a younger version of bucolic Will Shorthose, the ale-house keeper. The bare facts of Harry Akeham's life, which they had been tracing from his birth in that distant army camp, told them nothing of him.

By the time Harry walked into the ale-house, he had put on his shoes and stockings and tied his stock. 'Here's Harry,' said Will Shorthose, pushing open the door, and Harry himself seemed to have nothing to add to that. The two lawyers looked hard at him.

They saw a young man of middling height and slender build, with a pale skin and dark hair. Harry never had a high colour. Being much within doors kept him pale; that and the close confinement of the heated room in which his pupil lived. When he had the chance to be in the open air more than usual he tanned a pleasant light shade, without burning. His hair had lost the curliness of childhood, but it still waved slightly across his forehead. He had had no opportunity to develop the dashing, daring character of his father, though at times he showed his brightness and energy.

Since his schooldays, Harry's life had been constrained by circumstances he could not alter. He had, through what struggles no one would ever know, taught himself to accept his lot, and in the acceptance he had found happiness. He had also developed an inner strength which had combined with the sweetness of nature he had inherited from his mother. There was a great deal more to Harry than met the eye. However, at that moment in the dark confined room, it was only on what met the eye that he was judged.

His clothes, although they were neat and suited him, were shabby. He stood patiently waiting without fuss to hear what business they had with him, and the little twisted lawyer put him down as what had been expected, instead of what he really was.

'We are from the firm of lawyers Tillotson, Crump and Tillotson. I am Crump,' began the wizened man. He paused, but Harry showed no recognition of the name. 'And this is our invaluable Mr Robinson.' Harry inclined his head slightly in acknowledgement. 'If you are the person we believe you to be, we have made this journey to find you. Are you Mr Henry Akeham?'

'Yes, I am,' replied Harry, thus confounding Will Shorthose's opinions and confirming those of his wife in one short sentence.

Crump sighed in relief. 'We will ask you to prove that, of course. If you can do so satisfactorily we have news which may be of benefit to you. Could you, first of all, tell me of your parentage?

This is not a frivolous question, you understand, sir. Perhaps we could walk outside while we discuss it,' said Crump, who felt he could no longer bear the stuffy confines of the ale-house parlour.

Harry led the way and once outside the little man hunched his shoulders and looked fretful, thinking he could feel rain in the air. The three of them turned their steps to the left and walked along the grass at the side of the road. After a few yards Harry answered the question.

'You asked me about my parentage, sir. My father was Ensign Akeham of the Forty-third Foot; he was killed in action in ninety-seven. I hardly remember him. My mother is still living. The former clergyman in this village was her father and her name before she was married was Mollie Verity. Our home is that cottage straight across the green.'

'Is it possible for you to prove this?'

Whatever Harry felt at this rather sharply-put question, he answered with courtesy that his mother had copies of both her marriage lines and of the register entry of his baptism. 'Now that I have satisfied your curiosity, sir,' he went on, 'pray what do you want with me?'

'If you prove that you are what you say you are, young man,' the lawyer gave him a shrewd look, 'and we have no reason to doubt it, you are no longer Mr Henry Akeham.'

'Not myself? I don't see how I can be anybody else,' he replied.

'It is possible, however . . .' Crump looked down at his feet. 'It is possible that I am addressing the Earl of the Ainsty.'

'I beg your pardon, sir,' said Harry at last. 'I was not listening properly or I misunderstood . . . Could you . . .?'

'You know of course that the head of the Akeham family is the Earl of the Ainsty.'

Harry hesitated a little, then said, 'No, I did not know that. Perhaps I ought to explain. I know nothing of my father's family except that they are said to be prosperous. If you had come and told me that some small legacy had come my way from them I would have been surprised and delighted. But for you to talk of Earls is nonsense to me. I think we had better go and speak to my mother.'

They walked on before Crump said, 'The marriage was regarded, of course, as a misalliance.'

Harry's face darkened at this and Robinson, noticing it and

remembering that the mother of an Earl is not to be despised, interrupted, 'We will be delighted to meet your noble mother.'

Harry, who had not a pretentious bone in his body, was amused.

'How is it that you know nothing of your father's family?' asked Crump in a sharp tone, as though this were a fault or sin.

'I understand that they cast him off when he married my mother. Although the army chaplain wrote to acquaint them of my father's death in action, they offered no assistance to my mother in her need. We never mention them at home. It is as if my father were the only member of that family who ever existed. Shall we turn? My home is over there.'

They had reached the end of the green, where the high road left the village. They turned and slowly paced back along the opposite side to the ale-house until they reached the cottage. Only a shallow step separated its door from the ducks and geese which wandered freely on the grass. Harry opened the door to usher the strangers in.

The cottage had a single, largish room with a scullery at the back. A small fire was burning on the hearth and over it swung a copper kettle. The walls were limewashed sparkling white and the floor was of red bricks. The furniture was simple but there was a shelf full of Harry's books, and a sword which had belonged to his father hung on the wall. Mollie had come in from the garden and was sitting at the window, spinning a fine thread of linen on her wheel, while the tabby cat took its ease on a rug in front of the fire.

'We have guests, Mother.'

Mollie looked up, stopped her spinning, and came forward.

'May I introduce Mr Crump and Mr Robinson, lawyers. They have come in connection with Father's family.'

'Harry, I do not allow that family to be mentioned in this house,' said his mother, and she put her hand to her heart. 'They caused my dear husband too much distress. I do not wish to have anything to do with them.'

Harry's voice was gentle. 'Today must be an exception, Mother, because they have come specially, and you are too hospitable to turn them out into the rain . . .' For it had come on to rain again, as Crump had feared it might. The sky had darkened considerably during their brief turn around the village green and, as if to second Harry's words, raindrops now fell against the window and there was a growl of thunder and a flash of summer lightning.

Mollie's lips tightened a little, but she glanced at the window and made no protest when Harry drew chairs up for the visitors.

'Mother, did you know that the head of the Akeham family was the Earl of the Ainsty?' Mollie nodded. 'Mr Crump and Mr Robinson wish me to prove that I am my father's son. We can oblige them so far, can we not?' The bare idea that anyone should doubt it – for why was proof needed if there was not doubt? – ensured Mollie's co-operation.

'I'll fetch the papers,' she said and went to the door which opened on to a narrow stair built into the thickness of the wall. She went upstairs and could be heard moving about in the bedroom which lay above them. They could hear distinctly the sound of the lid of a chest being thrown back and a scuffling as its contents were moved about. There was constraint in the atmosphere until Mollie returned and handed some folded papers to Harry. They were the copies made for her by the clergymen who had carried out the ceremonies of marriage and baptism, together with some of Ensign Akeham's army papers.

'I think these are what you need,' she said, and after a brief glance Harry handed them on to Crump, who produced his own notes and compared the information with that supplied by Mollie. After a matter of minutes, he looked up. The end of the search brought a sense of relief.

'There is no doubt of it!' he exclaimed. 'May I greet you, my lord, in your proper title. You are the tenth Earl of the Ainsty.'

Harry, who was glad he was sitting down, drew in his breath sharply and looked at his mother. She caught at the arm of a chair before sinking into it, and after meeting his eyes for a brief moment, turned her head to look into the fire.

'Can you explain?' he asked, turning to Crump. The lawyer was only too ready to embark on lengthy explanations, and this gave Harry and his mother a little time to realize what was happening.

'Your great-grandfather was the fifth Earl of the Ainsty. He left two surviving sons and two daughters. You must realize that the estates are entailed on the male line, so the daughters and their children could not inherit. No female can inherit. At the time when your father ran away and joined the army, he was the younger son of a younger son. His uncle was married and in the process of rearing a nursery full of children, both sons and daughters. There appeared no chance at all of your father being in any way concerned with the succession. He was very much a cadet branch.' Harry nodded to show that he understood. 'Eventually your great-grandfather died, and his eldest son, your great-uncle, became the sixth Earl. Your father's family, you understand, had been provided with small fortunes of their own out of income, and they lived in a comfortable way. When you said they cut him off, that was true, as far as their own personal provision went. But even if the earldom had been at that time in their branch, there was nothing they could do to exclude him from his position in the line of succession to it. That was out of their power. Even if such an exclusion had been possible, they would never have thought of it because his chance seemed so remote.'

Mollie and Harry were both quietly listening, her eyes still on the fire, his on what he could see of her face.

'What happened next?' he asked.

'Your great-uncle was unlucky in his family. The sons died, some in infancy, some in early childhood, one or two as young men. He was left only with three daughters, who all married suitably. When he died, his brother, your grandfather, inherited as the seventh Earl. He was then an old man. His younger son, your father, had already died, and he had no contact with you or with your mother. His eldest son, the natural heir, was living, married, and had a son himself of about your age. There still seemed no possibility of your line being concerned in the earldom.'

'I take it,' said Harry, rather moved at hearing of these relatives, so nearly connected, whom he had never met or had the opportunity to know, 'that my grandfather himself is now dead? You do not come as his emissary?' This last question held a note of hope. He would have liked to think of his grandfather repenting of his harshness and wanting to know and help his mother and himself. He felt that he would have liked to meet his grandfather who had so unexpectedly become an earl, although it had never occurred to him until that moment. It might have been possible to revere the old gentleman, even to love him. Just then he glanced in his mother's direction and saw that this whole episode was giving her pain. He remembered that if he had agreed to be acquainted with those who had spurned her beloved husband it would have hurt her, and that he would never have done so. His regret vanished.

'Your grandfather died some five years ago, aged seventy-one. Your uncle became eighth Earl. He was, I regret to say, a man of intemperate habits, and was carried off by an apoplexy in his fiftieth year. That happened just twelve months ago.'

'And my cousin, a man, you said, of about my age, became Earl?'

'He became the ninth Earl and seemed set for a long and happy life.'

'What happened?'

'He was killed by a fall out riding a week ago. The horse rolled on top of him and he died shortly after.'

'It would seem to be an ill-omened thing, this earldom you are trying to give to me!'

'No! No!' Crump was excessively shocked. 'It is true that we have moved in twenty-five years from the fifth Earl, your great-grandfather, to yourself, the tenth. But three of those have died in their eighth decade of life and even your uncle was in his fifties. Had he been more temperate no doubt he would have been alive today and for many years to come. Even if his only son had predeceased him, he could have remarried and begotten more sons.'

'My cousin was the ninth Earl . . . What a deal of relatives I have acquired, even if they are dead ones.'

'Then, you know, it might have chanced that your cousin married young and left male children.'

'It might, indeed. In that case I would never, I suppose, have heard of their existence, or of all these grandfathers and great-grandfathers, intemperate uncles and married-off aunts.'

'Quite probably you would not,' replied Crump, who failed to understand Harry's state of mind.

'I could wish that they had all lived and been happy.'

Crump had to admit to himself that had he been in Harry's place, he would have been very pleased to hear of their deaths.

'You hear how the case is, Mother,' said Harry gently in an undertone to Mollie.

'Well,' said she, wiping a tear from her eye, 'and what is it to me? Those who were so cruel to your father are dead and that is an end of it.'

'Will it make no difference, Mother? You realize they say I am the next male heir? A title does not come unsupported, when the estates are entailed. We are not so humble and out of the way as not to know such things. Am I right in supposing property, Mr Crump, Mr Robinson?'

'There is . . .' Crump hesitated. 'There is some property, my lord.'

'It will mean comfort for you, Mother. Ease, in return for all the sacrifices you have made for me. A carpet for your floor and satin slippers for your feet.'

'I will not take them!' cried Mollie, and buried her head in her hands. 'I will take nothing from the Akeham family. You hear, Harry? Nothing. It would please me if you refused it.'

'You hear my mother?' Harry turned to Crump. 'It has been a pretty dream. You have diverted my fancy for an hour, sir. But you heard my mother, and I cannot hurt her. These benefits must be refused.'

Crump and Robinson gazed at him in astonishment, and Crump began to explain. 'It does not work in that way, my lord. At the moment of your cousin's death you became the tenth Earl. That is unalterable. The estates are entailed on the male line of which you are the last and sole representative. That is unalterable. You have not the choice of bearing or not bearing these honours and estates. The title must be passed on to your male heir or die with you. Nor can you alienate or sell the property. It has happened in my experience that a title has passed to a more remote relative than you are, in one case many generations removed from the parent stem. The only unusual feature in your case is that you were ignorant of the matter.'

'Mother, what am I to say to these gentlemen?'

Mollie lifted her face and dried her eyes on a handkerchief. 'You must do as you think best, Harry, but what was refused to my husband I wish to have no part in.'

'At least I can discover what is involved.' Harry was thoughtful.

'I will make tea,' said Mollie, moving the kettle.

'Will there be – when debts and funeral expenses and so on are settled – will there be any income left? One hears nowadays of so many impoverished noblemen.'

'There will be an ample income, my lord,' replied Crump in a severe tone, while Robinson choked and had to cover his mouth hastily. The 'country bumpkin' looked at him and drew his own conclusions.

'Will there be some kind of dwelling? You spoke of estates. A country house, an old hall or manor?'

Crump allowed his eyes to travel slowly round the one room of the cottage.

'There will be –' and his voice was dry with understatement '–there will be Ramillies, my lord.'

At the time, that word meant nothing to Harry.

Within the week, the whole of the landed gentry of the county in which Ramillies was situated knew that the next heir was found. From Lady Langbar in the north to the Marquis of Humber in the south, they were all busy with speculation.

Although George the Fourth's Queen, poor Caroline of Brunswick-Wolfenbüttel, had landed in England on the sixth of June without even an official residence being provided for her reception, in at least one county of her dominions the interest in her actions and her claim to title was all but overshadowed by the matter first raised in Langbar Hall during the incident of the very small mouse – the affair of the inheritance of Ramillies.

CHAPTER TWO

RAMILLIES

It took some time for Harry really to believe that he had, by this strange twist of fortune, inherited a title and estates. He felt that he hardly dared believe it. It seemed best – as his employer was away on holiday in any case – to go along with the two lawyers to London and gradually to find out the truth or otherwise of the matter.

Mollie had been very distressed. It had opened up old wounds, and he wondered if he even dared to buy her a present while he was away.

They went to London, and the formalities were gone through. What wholly convinced Harry was an amount of money pressed upon him by the bank used by previous Earls, with the assurance that it was only a fraction of the moneys which would be due to him.

The word got out somehow into the trading community, and Harry was amazed to find that London retailers were anxious to press on him all manner of luxuries quite without apparent thought of pecuniary reward. Tailors waited on the stairs to see him and dealers in *objets de virtu* besieged him on the steps. He refused them all, polite but puzzled and uncomfortable. Most of his time in London was spent in various dark chambers of banks and legal establishments being told things about his new rank and possessions which were all too much to take in at once.

In spite of Mollie's wishes, he purchased a plain warm cloak for her for the winter and a quantity of gloves, which he thought she would not refuse.

He arrived back in Cherry Wigston at the end of the week and she allowed herself to be persuaded to accept his gifts and to agree to his continuing to give her the same amount of money per year which he had previously been earning as a tutor. More she would not take, nor would she go with him to take possession of his estates, or refer to his new title. Harry could see that it was an upset which only time could help her over. Only time, too, could restore him to his usual self. For a week the delightful gaiety of his smile had hardly been seen. Usually when he turned his personality towards other people, they felt a strange reassurance, and never more so than when his eyes were laughing and his attitude full of relaxed joyousness. Then other people felt as they did when they saw the glow of firelight in winter, or heard the birds singing in spring. The world was safe and everything, instantly, was all right. His mother knew the feeling well, as did the boy he taught.

Now, though, his brightness was in eclipse. Perhaps after all it was some kind of dream! He only said to their relatives at the vicarage that he had come into a legacy from his father's family, and said the same to Will Shorthose.

Was it really true? Was he now someone of importance, even of grandeur? What would his estates be like? There was the sense of wonder and adventure . . . then there sometimes came over him a feeling of dread, almost of fear. A desire to be unobtrusive had always been part of his character.

Crump was to accompany him northward to Ramillies. The silent Robinson has been left behind in London. Harry found himself worrying over his little pupil and thought he would be able to adjust better to the change in his fortunes when he had freed his mind of anxiety on that score.

It was a wrench to write to his employer in Scarborough, giving up his post; he felt the qualm every hard-working young man must feel at giving up a secure and hard-won employment for an uncertain adventure. Then he found that one of his old friends would be able to take the position and he wrote to recommend him, enclosing an affectionate letter for his ex-pupil. Then there was no other excuse to put off the journey to Ramillies . . .

On the Ramillies estate was the village of Anby, which had in it a small school. This school was taught by a demure, capable young woman, Hannah Clare. She had come into the village a couple of years before and to most of the people living there she was as much a stranger still. The village school had been created as a sewing school by one of the Countesses, some fifty years before. Regulations for a uniform of brown woollen, with white caps and tippets, and warm, hooded red cloaks had been laid down then and never altered since. The girls made their own outfits as part of their training. The countryside round about was very proud of the skills of the sewing school and the girls were snapped up by various employers when they left.

During the time of the fifth Earl, he had added to the cares of the school mistress by asking her to take charge also of the smaller boy children, up to the age of seven or eight years. Then they were considered too strong and rumbustious for petticoat government. If they were clever, they walked to the school in the nearest town, and if they were not, they started work with their fathers in the fields. While they were in Hannah's charge in school, they too wore brown woollen, in the form of breeches and jackets, with white bands.

Hannah Clare had the use of the neat little house at the end of the single-storied, Gothick-windowed school, and complete independence of action as long as she had the approval of the current Earl.

The news of the advent of the tenth Earl ran across the estate like wind over water. Every inhabitant knew exactly when the great black travelling carriage had set out to meet him on his journey north and just when he could be expected to arrive. It seemed to Hannah that it would be both prudent and expedient to have her school children lined up at the roadside, waiting to wave a greeting when the new arbiter of their several fates drove past in splendour. Being as efficient as she was beautiful, Hannah had them there in good time. Previous Earls and Countesses had never changed the rules governing dress at the school, so the line of children and teacher presented a quaint appearance. The russet-brown dresses, white caps and tippets, and red cloaks were of the same pattern they had always been. If Hannah were worried about being fifty years behind the times in her dress, she never let anyone know it. People smiled when they saw the school, in pure pleasure at the quaint, comely orderliness, at the bright faces of the children, the grace of the older girls and the good looks of Hannah herself. The outdated costumes set them apart and they felt that they were very special.

The change in Harry's life was never more apparent than when, on his journey north with Crump, they changed over from hired conveyances to the carriage which belonged to the Earls of the Ainsty. A flunkey in plum-coloured velvet, liberally laced with silver, conducted him to the vehicle and bowed as he let down the steps for Harry's august feet to use when climbing into it. The new Earl stood still on the pavement, ignoring both flunkey and Crump. He took in the full glory of richly-embroidered hammer-cloth, gleaming varnish, panels emblazoned with a coat of arms; then he walked past the carriage and its attendants to where the horses stood waiting. There were four of them, grey, and he walked slowly to their heads where a young groom in livery stood at the noses of the leaders.

Every inch of harness shone with polishing, as did the horses themselves, patient, powerful creatures. Harry smiled at the groom, patted the nose of the nearest horse, and went thoughtfully back to the carriage door and the waiting lawyer. The whole retinue had been holding their breath, wondering if they would satisfy his eye or if there would be some complaint.

It was on stepping into that noble carriage for the first time that Harry began to realize what he had become. The door closed on him and Crump; the attendants moved to their several places; the command was given; the whole assortment of men, horses, wheels, squeaked and clattered into movement. Harry reckoned that with outriders, grooms, coachmen, there were ten able-bodied men and nearly as many horses conducting his formerly insignificant self into his new life.

Those same ten men, as the whole cavalcade swept in a regal manner through the flat plain of the centre of the county of broad acres, were for their part considering Henry, Lord Ainsty. No word of censure had been spoken. So far at least, they could assume that their efforts to please had been successful. He was not taller than ordinary, nor fatter than ordinary, and he was, for an Earl, very badly dressed, but his smile – they had all seen that rather small and uncertain smile, but distinctly one of Harry Akeham's – his smile had in a few seconds put them all on his side, and ensured that their journey to Ramillies had an air of reassurance and hope. Every Earl had his own distinctive qualities. There had been the Bold Earl, the Mad Earl, the Shepherd Earl, the Building Earl. There was speculation about this one. In that first few minutes the omens were felt to be good.

The day was already drawing towards late afternoon and the school-children had been waiting by the roadside for half an hour. It was a dark day, unseasonably cold and cruel weather for June. Hannah almost told them to put on their red cloaks, but that seemed extreme for what was nominally a summer afternoon. They shivered and put their hands inside their white cuffs. The rain threatened, and a sprinkle of fine drops dampened them, but it blew over again, and they hoped for a little sun. Hope was abroad on the Ramillies estate that day.

The carriage had been driving along an undulating, pleasant road for some time when the rocking of turning a corner and a different sound coming from the wheels made Harry realize that some change had taken place. He had almost been dozing. Now he sat forward hastily and looked out of the window. They had swept from the main road on to the smaller road leading to Ramillies.

'Are we there?' asked Harry.

It was unfortunate that Harry and Crump did not enjoy being in each other's company. Crump had not liked having to be so long away from London, had thought Harry ill-dressed, and during Harry's period of shock at their news had decided that he was oafish. Harry in his turn did all he could to be courteous to the snappy little lawyer and not to mind the snide remarks which Crump could not help making.

'We are just entering your property.'

Harry was looking intently out of the window. He opened it, slid down the glass and put out his head. Looking forward with eagerness, he saw a road straight as a ruler, leading uphill. There is not in all England a straighter road. No sooner had they swept to the top of a rise, all hoofbeats and clatter, than a further stretch of ruler-straight road and another hill lay in front of them. 'All this mine?' thought Harry, looking at the splendid clumps of beech trees to left and right. The whole rural scene around was one of great beauty and the road had a prophetic quality, as though it were preparing the minds of those who travelled on it for some great event.

Grey-gold stone came into sight, forming an archway over the road. The stone was rough and rubble like, as though it had been thrown up by giants.

'This is the gateway, I suppose.'

'Not yet, my lord.'

The road was pressed upon by the walls up to the arch, with their towers, turrets and small pyramids. The mounted attendants on either side fell back until the carriage had cleared the opening, then came through themselves and galloped quickly up. Ahead the road lay ruler-straight still. Crowning the next rise were fortifications like the outworks of a castle, walls with bastions and towers at intervals. Harry saw them almost with horror. For an instant he imagined a great crumbling keep, a decayed portcullis, bat-haunted towers. Then he saw that the road, not deflecting an inch, led straight through these fortifications. Between the bobbing heads of horses and men he could see that the road led to yet another arch, surmounted by a pyramid, and with a row of windows on either side. He had heard of houses built actually over a road. This must be one such.

'That is the house, I take it.'

'That is the gatehouse.'

'Of course,' said Harry, trying not to sound surprised and turning again to look out of the window. The gatehouse grew closer and once more the road (although not a whit narrower in fact) seemed almost to pinch itself together to penetrate the thick heaviness of the stone buildings. The sky had been darkening ominously for some time and a scatter of raindrops was hurled sideways at the carriage, while a strong wind, growing in force, caused the trees to moan and bend before it. The noise of horses and wheels was intensified as they pierced the arch under the mass of stone.

They came out to be confronted with one last rise. Crowning it was an obelisk; simple, yet utterly grand in its serenity, soaring upward through the massy greenness of the straining, weeping trees as though it would reach the dull grey arch of heaven. Harry was dumb with wonder. Not even the miles of road, not even the fantastic and noble outworks, nor the grand width and breadth of all the country round, had prepared him for the impact of that obelisk. It was a hundred feet of sheer stone, plain, unornamented except by the subtlety of interaction of vertical and near-vertical, the impact of cream stone on grey sky and green trees, the magnificence of a statement so simple that a child might have made it yet so powerful that it took one of the greatest of architectural thinkers to imagine it and place it there.

As the horses strained their way upward towards the obelisk, Harry caught sight of a flutter of white and brown at its foot.

'There are people there,' he said.

'From the estate, I have no doubt,' replied Crump. Then, with a helpfulness he rarely showed, 'They will be pleased if you wave and acknowledge them.' Harry started a little at the thought that complete strangers would be pleased if he waved at them, but the friendliness of it appealed to him and he leaned forward ready to do it.

They reached the foot of the obelisk and it seemed to vanish out of sight into the heavens, leaving only the solidity of its base to reassure mere mortal men. Around it was a wide sweep of road. Even this road, adept as it was at ignoring outworks which could have been built by gods, had to bend to this authority. The road acknowledged superiority in the grand manner, sweeping in a magnificent circle round the plinth.

Here, in a row on the grass bordering the road, were waiting Hannah Clare and her school children, a petty row of irregular, varied, individual human beings in contrast to the super-human majesty of the obelisk. They all had something white in their hands to wave.

'Slow down!' cried Harry suddenly to the coachman, who was so much astonished that he did so instantly. As the grand cavalcade slowed, wheeling on the circular road, Harry waved cordially to the little assembly. One and all, Hannah and the children waved back, flapping their white cloths and handkerchiefs and crying out in an irregular kind of way, 'Hurrah!'

The boys were in russet-brown breeches and jackets, with white bands round their necks falling in square-ended rectangles of white on to their russet-brown chests; they were in front of the older girls, whose job it was to keep them in order. Harry, thrown into a new situation and the uncongenial society of Crump, was nostalgic for the sound of children's voices and the squeak of slate pencils. He met Hannah's eyes as the carriage passed, and she was smiling her expedient smile. In that moment he became prepossessed towards her. Drawing his head inside the carriage again, he observed to the lawyer, 'They are a credit to their teacher.'

'Very commendable.'

Looking out of the window again, he saw that the clumps of beech had given way to serried ranks of limes which were suffering just as much at the hands of the dark, boisterous wind. After wheeling round the axis of the obelisk they were now moving at right angles to their previous route and he saw an extensive block of buildings ahead. Not liking the hint of disparagement in Crump's replies to his questions, he said nothing. This produced a remark made by Crump with some civility, that they were about to pass the stables. Seeing a line of stable hands obviously waiting, Harry leaned out and waved to them too. Ahead was a mass of stone buildings so large that after one glimpse he did not look again. He kept his head inside the carriage and wondered what was to come.

The carriage slowed down and took another right turn, then drew up inside a hollow square, three sides of which were formed by massive buildings of stone. The fourth side was open to a breathtaking stretch of serene short grass spreading down to a great lake in the middle distance. The water shone like a shield of grey steel. On either side, arms of woodland reached out to embrace it and, beyond, the countryside melted into distant greyness to meet the cloudlike hills on the horizon.

The wind summoned its forces and threw a charge of raindrop javelins across the landscape. The flunkey jumped down from the coach and ran to put down the steps and open the door. Here in the shelter of the stone wings of the house the wind was partly foiled.

'We have arrived at Ramillies, my lord,' said Crump.

Harry climbed down past the bowing flunkey and looked up the two short flights of steps to the front door. 'It is not a house,' he thought, as soon as he was able to think at all. 'It is a palace of unexampled grandeur . . .'

On either side of the open door the household staff were waiting in line to bob their curtsies and bow their bows of greeting. A little behind Harry, Crump was heard to murmur, 'Your servants, my lord,' and the house-steward, standing with great dignity at one side of the door, said to Harry, 'May I welcome you to Ramillies, my lord.'

'He was a nobody,' said Lady Langbar, passing her lord a cup of coffee. 'No background, no training. His mother was a daughter of the vicarage' – she made that sound slightly reprehensible – 'and his father only a junior line.'

'The blood will be there, you know,' replied Lord Langbar, who had returned late the previous evening from a short visit to a distant property of his. Laetitia watched him with concern. He was too like her mother for comfort. Her mother had tired easily and died young, and watching her mother's brother, Laetitia feared in case he too was taken from her. She stood a little in awe of him but still cherished every line of the aristocratic head, made dominating by its high-bridged nose, and sensitive by its hooded, clear grey eyes.

Lord Langbar was just then deciding whether or not to embark upon the conquest of a lightly-boiled egg.

'You think blood will tell, my dear,' went on Lady Langbar, 'and you are always right in these matters. There are the six thousand acres, too, and Ramillies. It would be worth marrying him for those, whatever his drawbacks.' Her eye was resting on Laetitia, who blushed and began to pleat her napkin into folds. 'One would not wish to take anyone quite impossible into the family, of course,' conceded Lady Langbar in conclusion.

'It would be just the match for Letty,' said his lordship, knocking his egg decisively over the head with a spoon.

'He sounds too dreadful, Mama,' put in Bella. 'You cannot expect Laetitia to marry anyone like that.'

'He was the tutor of the crippled child of a tradesman in a market town in the Midlands.'

After a mouthful of bread and butter, Lord Langbar remarked that he had heard that the new Earl had insisted, before travelling north to take possession of Ramillies, on finding a new tutor for the boy.

'You see he had no sense of proportion,' exclaimed Lady Langbar in disgust. 'As if it mattered what became of the boy. He did not know what was proper to a man of rank.'

Laetitia had brightened. 'Did he find another tutor for the boy, Uncle?'

'Your uncle will not know! I should hope the man soon turned his thoughts to something more to the point.'

'The whole county will be welcoming him,' remarked Lord Langbar to his egg.

'Yes. We must give a dinner. Another slice of ham, Bella?'

'I have finished, thank you, Mama. Will people be giving balls in his honour?'

'Hardly at this time of year. You will get the usual ones during race week in August. Probably you young people will roll up the carpets and have a country dance on a few evenings.'

'He will have to return hospitality. Do you remember a twelvemonth ago, Letty, the lovely evening we had at Ramillies? When the ninth Earl inherited? What an outstanding occasion that was. Everything done in such a handsome style.'

'I did not enjoy it,' Laetitia could not stop herself saying in her quiet voice.

Her Aunt's retrospective wrath, fearsome even after twelve months, showed signs of descending on her.

'I should think you did not enjoy it, my girl! Behaving in that absurd way. Anyone would think your Uncle and I had been about to compel you to marry the man whether you liked it or not. Let us hope we see a more proper attitude in the future.'

'Of all matches for you, Lord Ainsty would be the most desirable,' put in Lord Langbar mildly. 'Your rank is equal, your estates march together. This new man is young, I believe. Though so was the ninth Earl. It was not inequality of age that you disliked in him, Letty.'

'I could not bear him,' replied Letty in a low voice.

'Well, I hope you will not take any of your silly dislikes to this man. Try to be amiable.'

'You can be very charming, my dear, when you try to please. Your Aunt finds it hard work when you will not grant her your co-operation. Do not forget she is doing her best for you.'

'Yes, Uncle,' replied the Countess of Elmet.

'I will ride over to call the day after tomorrow when I have business in Malton. What day will suit you, my love, to receive him as our dinner guest?'

'Wednesday,' said Lady Langbar with instant decision. 'Although any day next week would do. Preferably Wednesday; that will give us time to prepare something elegant.'

Whatever he had been in the past, he was now the Earl of the Ainsty, and Lady Langbar was determined to honour him accordingly.

CHAPTER THREE

The School

Harry Akeham stepped into the hall of his new possession, Ramillies, and audibly caught his breath in wonder. Around a vast extent of stone floor with dark and pale slabs set diamond-wise, stately columns rose to support springing arches, which in turn supported a high dome.

Crump, behind him, sniffed in disapproval. He disliked architecture which made him feel so clearly his own smallness and unimportance. The hall of Ramillies reminded him of St Paul's. The statues and frescoes looming above him made him long to scuttle round the edge of the floor like a frightened crab.

Harry, in contrast, felt his spirit uplifted. Here had been at work the mind of a man who could join gaiety to grandeur. A man who could dizzily uplift a majestic dome, and, pretending that his daring feat had in reality reached the skies and intercepted the sun itself, could line the dome with a painting showing the horses of the sun galloping down from heaven. They seemed about to tumble into the airy space below them.

This man's wit could not be suppressed. He took heavy stone and while leaving it full of nobility made it vibrate with life and joy. The hall was silent around Harry, yet it seemed to him that it was full of fantasy, colour and movement.

Crump cleared his throat with a scraping noise like the opening of a door and said, 'It is usually considered a masterpiece.'

'Everyone must consider it so,' said Harry, with reverence in his voice.

'Yes – yes –' Crump looked down at his feet. 'What time do you wish to dine, my lord?'

'At whatever time is usual.'

'It is for you to say.'

Not for the first time, Harry felt impatient and irritated with the lawyer. At this moment could he not have been left alone briefly, to absorb this wonderful place without being asked about dinner? Crump had taken charge of such arrangements on the journey and Harry wished he had gone on doing so a little longer. However, he spoke pleasantly as usual. 'We have been travelling for an age, it seems. Should we have dinner as soon as it can conveniently be ready?'

Crump turned to the housekeeper, who was hovering in the background. 'The Earl wishes to dine immediately. Will you wish to change your clothing, my lord?' – this to Harry.

Harry was regretting his negative responses to the obliging tailors of London. His clothing, he realized, was not in keeping for a man in his new position. Everything he had was neat and serviceable for a tutor but in no manner fitting for a nobleman. Then, for the first time, Harry showed signs of taking command of the new situation he was in. 'We will not change tonight,' he said decisively. 'A wash, though, would be welcome.'

'I would like to explain,' said the house-steward with an apologetic cough, 'that recent Earls have not been using the state bedrooms. Of course, if your lordship wishes, we can make them ready quickly, but a room considered more convenient and comfortable has been in use lately . . .'

'That will do very well,' replied Harry, and was shown to a luxurious bedroom where a manservant was waiting. Cans of hot water appeared. In half an hour Harry, feeling both rested and confident, went downstairs again and was shown into the dining-room at the east side of the hall. There he partook of a long, uneasy meal, with Crump at the other end of a very large table, some two miles away down an expanse of shimmering damask. It was a relief to retire into the saloon, a greater relief still when, having been seated in virtual silence for an hour, one each side of the fireplace, Crump asked his permission to leave in the morning. Then Harry would be quite alone among strangers, but surely it could be no worse than this ghastly evening.

As soon as he decently could, Harry went to bed, and surrounded by grandeur, fell gratefully asleep.

The following morning he said goodbye to the lawyer and was left by himself in his great house, wondering what on earth Earls did with themselves when they were not either eating or sleeping.

The high wind and interrupted rain of the previous day had died away and been succeeded by a mist almost like low cloud, which obscured the view from the windows. There was a vague impression of greenness sweeping from the house and of a general dewiness in the air, betraying itself by a film of droplets on the outside of the glass of the closed windows.

Harry was feeling bemused by it all and could hardly believe that he was the owner of such a building as Ramillies. He wanted to be quiet and by himself to think about it and to explore without an escort of servants, so he told the house-steward exactly that. Everyone was told that they were not to be seen on any account, with the rather eerie result that Harry several times saw a disappearing plum-coloured livery or a skirt of modest cut and subdued colour vanishing through one doorway as he entered at another.

The magnificent hall was on the north side of the block of building. To right and left from it led a long corridor, the antique gallery, backing the main suite of rooms. These were intercommunicating so that Harry could pass from one to another without using the corridor, and they lay along the south front of the building.

As he explored, he found that the saloon where he had sat with Crump and the dining-room where they had eaten were only two of this suite, though they were perhaps the grandest. Each room had silk curtains and superb furniture. The walls were decorated with tapestries, paintings, mirrors, in profusion.

When he found a square piano and a pile of music, he decided he must be in the music room, and the musical instruments in the plasterwork confirmed this. Another room was the state bedroom and as he looked in wonder at the lofty fourposter bed with a set of steps to climb up into it, he was glad that he was not expected to sleep there.

Harry rather enjoyed himself, though he felt a little like Gulliver in the land of the giants. But after a while he began to feel lonely and isolated. It was at this point that he had gone off at right-angles to the suite of rooms along the garden front, and he opened the door into what was evidently the library and found another human being there.

Harry almost cried out in relief as he saw the bookcases lining the room from floor to ceiling. He was beginning to think that none of his ancestors shared his tastes. It was a dim room, for it depended on north light. Harry walked into the congenial atmosphere, rested his weight on an inlaid satinwood table and prepared to gaze round at leisure – and then found that he was not alone. A grey man seemed almost to materialize. He was about Harry's own height, wearing a coat and breeches of silvery grey, and with grey hair. He was leaning against the bookcases in a dark corner and had a book open in his hand.

The man marked his place in his book with his finger and looked back at Harry. Neither of them spoke at first, then Harry felt that he must break the silence. He advanced, holding out his hand. 'Allow me to introduce myself: I am Harry Akeham.' Too late, he realized that he probably ought to have said, 'I am Lord Ainsty,' and felt in the wrong.

The other man smiled an odd, twisted smile. 'I am Peregrine Akeham, milord,' he said, and put out his hand to meet Harry's. It was a cold, thin hand.

'Are you one of the family?' asked Harry, surprised. 'Lud, I thought they were all dead.'

'They have often wished I were, I dare say.'

'What relation are you to me?'

'Some kind of cousin,' answered Peregrine, not caring to be more informative. 'They said that you wanted to be alone and that all the servants were to keep out of the way. That could hardly apply to me.'

'I should say not!' cried Harry genially. 'It gives me great pleasure to acquire a relative. Come over here, let us talk by the window. It is a damned dull sort of day, hardly light enough in here to read.' His instinctive kindness, assuming Peregrine to be a poor relation, brought out a warmth of welcome.

Peregrine advanced into the light and Harry, transferring his weight from the satinwood table to the window shutters, leaned there and took a good look at him. Akeham was older than himself. His face showed age, and on one side of it was a long, puckering line of scar tissue. Battle, or at least a duel, thought Harry.

'If you wish, I will go to live somewhere else,' remarked Peregrine. 'I have always existed here under the merest toleration, and am prepared to leave on the instant.' He could have said nothing better calculated to ensure that Harry would always be quite unable to ask him to go.

But although Harry smiled and there was complete reassurance in it, he did not instantly say, 'Of course you must stay!' Instead, he asked, 'What would you do if you left here?'

'I have friends. There are posts I could fill.'

'What posts? What have you been doing while you lived here? Mr Crump did not mention you to me.'

'Crump wouldn't!' And Peregrine's tone placed Crump with the worms. 'How long have I lived here? I was born here. What have I been doing so far? After a misspent youth, I came back to look after the library and muniment room.'

'You like books, antiquities, things of that kind?'

'Like? Can you have been a tutor and use such a lukewarm adjective?'

Harry grinned ruefully. 'Books have always been the breath of life to me. They are the channel through which we can commune with great minds. Yet . . .' and Harry looked away from Peregrine and gazed thoughtfully out of the window. 'Yet with all its drawbacks, life – pulsating life, erroneous, varied life – is in itself a book to be learned from.'

'It is just now opening before you,' and there was some friendliness in Peregrine's cold tones. 'Now you have found me, what do you intend to do with me?'

'Celebrate,' replied Harry promptly. 'Celebrate the finding of a relative and a companion. I was feeling the need of someone who knows the ways of the house. I feel as chilled this morning as if it were winter, and long for the comfort of a hot drink. I was wondering if it would upset the cook if I ordered tea? You and I must share it in token of our cousinship.'

Peregrine smiled. 'You have only to request it, milord.'

'They have lit a fire in the saloon. Shall we go there? Why have you no fire in the library?'

'Between March and November very few fires are lit and dependants do not ask for them.'

'Fudge! This penetrating damp will harm the books just as much in June as in December. I imagine the estate can afford it. I will order a fire at once. And tea – or perhaps coffee –'

'Cook usually makes some excellent wigs in the mornings.'

'Then that is settled.' The two men walked through the succession of beautiful rooms back to the saloon and up to the fire. Harry opened the door into the hall and found a footman sitting there. 'Coffee, please, and wigs,' he said briskly. 'And please tell the steward that you may all move about normally again. And send someone to light a fire in the library. There is to be a fire in there each day while this damp weather lasts.' Profoundly pleased at his boldness in giving his first orders, he turned back into the saloon and said, 'I am still at the stage of finding it a little nonsensical that I am the tenth Earl.'

'Oh, it is not nonsense.' Peregrine gave a sardonic, twisted smile. 'I keep the records and if anyone knows I do. There is no doubt as to your succession. And as the Earl, you are free to behave in any way you wish. You will soon get used to it.'

'Now how can that be?' cried Harry.

'Is it not obvious?'

Harry shook his head.

'You are the absolute authority. If you wish to dine at ten in the morning, then so be it. If you wish to go to bed in your top-boots, then that is your taste and after you are dead men will recount it as an interesting aspect of lordly behaviour.'

'I have no desire to go to bed in my boots,' smiled Harry.

'Anything else, then. You could shut up this house and live in London, never coming here again. You could eschew London and live here for the rest of your life. You could marry a countess or a dairymaid. There is none to say you nay.'

'It seems to me that such freedom is not good for a man,' said Harry uneasily. 'There must be duties as well as freedoms.'

'If I have your permission to speak frankly –'

'You have.'

'You asked about duties. You have responsibilities for all the beings who live on your revenues and therefore rely on you. The inhabitants of this house and estate, for instance.'

'Yes . . . I ought to get to know them all; their needs, their anxieties.' Harry looked brighter, and the footman arrived with a tray of coffee. Harry crumbled one of Cook's wheaten three-cornered wigs between his fingers and nibbled it, finding it to be delicious, straight from the oven. 'A brandy would go well with this coffee,' he added reflectively, and Peregrine darted off, to reappear with a decanter and two glasses.

'You probably did not eat well at breakfast with that old death's head opposite to you,' he remarked.

'I do not think I will ever eat well in that room.'

'The large state dining-room? Why not use the small dining-room? It is usual when the family are alone.'

'Why could Crump not have told me? Where do you eat, cousin?'

'In my room. I prefer it. Oh, we dependants have our little comforts. My privacy is one of them. Yours to command, though.'

'Cousin, to the future!' They drank slowly.

'Privacy,' said Harry after a while, pondering. He had been evolving schemes to do good to his dependants in his head, but Peregrine's words had made him aware of at least one danger. 'It might be difficult to combine helping my dependants with leaving them their privacy.'

'You will not be allowed yours. In one respect at least, your most intimate concerns will be regarded as public property, milord.'

'Oh? In what respect?'

'Local society will think you are in need of a Countess. They will all be calling on you to put forward their daughters, hoping you will favour one or the other.'

Harry finished eating his wig and drinking his coffee and returned to sipping the glass of brandy, reflecting that for the first time in his life he was in the position where he could contemplate matrimony and that if he had not come across Peregrine he would now have been feeling very lonely and a wife would have seemed an excellent thing. He avoided the subject by taking refuge in frivolity.

'Have I any other relatives about the house? Any ancient aunts, stray nephews or unknown grandmothers? Dare I go down into the cellars or up into the attics without falling over my kin?'

'I am the only one of the family here. You have other relatives of course – the Misses Godwin for instance – you will meet them soon enough.'

A hazy sunlight had for some time been brightening the cloud-like dampness of the morning and Harry felt restless now that he was internally comforted.

'Perhaps I will walk out,' he said. 'Or ride,' remembering the host of men and horses who had escorted him to Ramillies. 'Can you suggest a destination for me, cousin?'

'If you want responsibility, milord, ride to the village and call on the cottagers. They will appreciate the courtesy. Also, it would set minds at rest if you were to call at the school. It is only supported by your bounty and there are fears that the support may be discontinued.'

Harry remembered the line of children fluttering white handkerchiefs and the tall, good-looking school-mistress whose eyes had met his. He nodded.

'Then if you wish to ride further, a few miles away is the church where your more remote ancestors are buried. That might interest you. The Akeham who went on the Crusades lies there, and the Elizabethan Akeham who built a hall on this site long before this building was thought of.'

'Will you come with me, Peregrine?'

'If you wish it.'

Apart from occasionally riding his uncle the vicar's quiet old nag, Harry had no experience of riding, so he asked the footman to have two hacks brought round from the stables. The two men mounted and rode away from glorious Ramillies. Harry felt great relief. The place and situation in which he found himself were overpoweringly new and strange. To put it all away for a while, to trot in the strengthening sunlight which played softly on the flanking trees, and to reflect that he had all the time in the world to grow used to things, was bliss to him. They rode as far as the obelisk and then turned right. Harry was happy to have Peregrine's company; he felt there to be a tie of blood between them, something warm and full of meaning. They soon reached the village of Anby where Harry felt at home at once. It was not so very different from Cherry Wigston at first sight, though that had been a Midland village of independent yeomen and cottagers, and this was an estate village – his estate.

People appeared at cottage doors and in gardens, and their first shyness vanished in the warmth of Harry's smile. He chatted first to one and then to another, was asked into a cottage where the old wife was bedridden, and into another where a young wife was a-bed with her first child. Harry pressed a half sovereign into the tiny, waving palm of the infant.

The School

At the first moment of arriving in the village, Harry had been aware of the school and the school-house, but the people who came out to speak to him took up so much time that they were left until last. He accepted the offer of one of his own employees to share his noonday bread and cheese, and sat at the white scrubbed table with the family. Peregrine had refused this repast. 'I think not, milord,' he had said, and Harry had not quite liked the smile with which he said it, but had taken him at his word and left him on the green, minding the horses.

Hannah Clare had of course heard that they were in the village. One of her scholars who had a good view through the window had been keeping her posted of their progress and she had time to prepare. When, in the early afternoon, the two men appeared at the open door, at a gesture from her all the children rose to their feet and began to sing.

Harry was surprised and touched. He stood listening until the song was ended, then thanked the children and asked Hannah if the rest of the day could be granted to them as a holiday. The whole school shrieked with pleasure.

'With your permission, of course, Miss Clare,' he added, turning to her with a charming smile and his tone that of one teacher to another.

While he had been listening to the children he had been struck by their pleasant appearance and even more impressed by Hannah herself. She was certainly a very personable young woman! The antique dress, which any fashionable young lady would have died rather than wear, suited her. It brought out the unique quality of her looks. To Harry she seemed unspoilt and straightforward, dignified and serene.

'All say thank you to Lord Ainsty,' she commanded.

'Thank you, my lord,' they chorused, smiling faces above the white bands and tippets.

'I will come again to hear your lessons,' he promised, 'but now off with you all, so that I can talk to your teacher.' He was looking forward to talking to Hannah.

The small boys led the tumult out of the door. The oldest girls lingered, tidied their desks and admired Harry with little glances from the corner of their eyes, showing no haste to run after their younger brothers and sisters.

Harry had become infatuated with Hannah before the last child was out of the door. He and Peregrine moved to the middle of the simple schoolroom to chat to her. They stood among the benches for the small children and the desks for the senior girls. Hannah was above the middle height of women and her clear grey eyes looked directly into Harry's. They were the kind which look very fine when surrounded by quantities of black lashes and surmounted by level dark brows. Harry thought her the beau-ideal of a village schoolmistress.

'You need have no fears for the future of your school,' he said at once in his friendly way. 'I am delighted that it exists and look forward to many visits to it.'

'You must not always grant a holiday, or I will never be able to do any teaching,' said Hannah in a low musical voice, and smiled.

'I am sure other holidays must have been granted in the past. Did not my late cousin, the ninth Earl, do so?'

'Hm, hm,' said Peregrine in a warning voice, taking out a snuff-box and tapping it. 'Do you indulge, milord?'

Harry's words certainly seemed to have had a strange effect on Hannah. At his mention of the ninth Earl she had flinched and looked away and raised her hand to her forehead. It flashed across his mind that she was feeling faint. But whatever it was, she recovered herself quickly and looked back at him.

'No doubt on his first visit the ninth Earl may have done so – I really do not remember. On subsequent ones he certainly did not.'

'Very well, then,' said Harry good-temperedly. 'I must take care not to upset the work of the school too much. It will be a pleasure to come in from time to time.' Had the ninth Earl been intrusive, then? Had he been forever calling? If it had been so, she could not have liked it. He must remember to find out more about his cousin, the ninth Earl – no one had really spoken of him at all. Whatever he had or had not been, he must not be allowed to intrude on this budding acquaintanceship. The conversation of Miss Clare would mean much to him. In his former life, had he been a little better paid, she would have been the very wife for him. Why not still, wondered Harry? For although he had seen her for the first time on the previous day and had now been only half an hour in her presence, he felt it a very agreeable one and was willing to hazard any possible effect it might have on him if they were often together.

For the next half hour Hannah, Harry and Peregrine talked on the subject of education, and Harry studied Hannah's character as well as he could when those black-lashed eyes and clear complexion were close to him. Externally she was very calm and controlled and he wondered if he had imagined her slight distress earlier. She certainly seemed something of a snow maiden; but he suspected that under the snow was fire.

They prepared to go. 'I would appreciate frequent reports on your scholars,' Harry remarked. 'Will you not visit Ramillies to tell me of their progress? Then you could drink tea with my cousin and myself. No doubt I could send a conveyance to fetch you.'

'You do me honour, sir,' she said, with no tone in her voice which could tell him whether she was pleased or no. Harry, who had fallen so rapidly into some kind of love, could not stop himself pursuing the matter.

'Tomorrow is Saturday. You will not keep school in beyond twelve?'

'They are released at twelve.'

'Then I will expect you in the afternoon. Shall I send a carriage?'

'Oh, no!' cried Hannah. 'It is only a step. I have walked twenty times farther many a time without the slightest fatigue. We can walk to the house from here in half an hour.' She showed them to the door, and a smile betrayed the fact that those calm cheeks possessed two bewitching dimples.

'You astound me, milord,' said Peregrine as they rode away. 'Your quiet appearance hides such spirit. I rather think Miss Clare has taken your fancy.'

Harry laughed selfconsciously. 'She has, cousin. I have never met anyone who, on such short acquaintance, so nearly approached my ideal.'

'She has the reputation of being a cold and reserved young woman.'

Harry felt as though he were being warned, but only laughed and said, 'With those dimples?' and began to ask Peregrine questions about the country they were riding through. They were still riding away from Ramillies. It had been decided that they would go as far as the church which housed the early monuments of the Akehams. This lay close to the high road between York and the coast, near a village some three miles from Anby.

When it had been built, in the year twelve hundred, the church had been the centre of a thriving settlement, but it had long since ceased to be the centre of anything except green fields, the village having, with some lack of consideration, removed itself half a mile off. The ancient building now lay isolated on a side road.

Halfway there, Peregrine slowed his horse and then came to a halt. He leaned back, looking very tired and worn. Harry, turning his horse and coming back to him, blamed himself for lack of consideration. While he had refreshed himself in the labourer's cottage, the older man had waited outside. Not only Peregrine's hair and coat were grey. His face too had the grey look which is the result of strain and weakness. 'You are tired. It was thoughtless of me. I have been keeping you waiting for me, looking after both horses, and now riding further.'

Peregrine smiled a half-amused and half-sardonic smile.

'It has been a pleasure to me. But, with your permission, I will now turn back. The church is beyond those trees ahead of you. It would, after all, be more fitting if you went alone to your first meeting with your ancestors. They are my ancestors too but my face has long been familiar to them. I will ride back slowly and you will catch me up, I daresay. Even if you do not you can hardly miss your way back to Ramillies.'

'No. There is no danger of that. Do go, good cousin. Would you order dinner? What hour has been customary in the house?'

'Shall we say half-past six? I will.' Peregrine turned and rode off slowly. Harry pressed on in the direction of the church, glad to be alone. He reflected that as he sat there exhausted, Peregrine had looked like an old roué. What was his full story, Harry wondered? His head was whirling with all the new sensations of the last twenty-four hours. Visiting a church and tombs would no doubt calm him.

Arriving at the church, he slid from the saddle and led the horse through into the churchyard. Once he had closed the gate it would be safe enough. Leaving it to browse, he walked over to the low church door of oaken planks patterned with iron bolts. Turning the stiff handle, he swung the door inwards and moved forward – and it was all he could do to stop himself from entering headlong. Luckily he still had his grasp on the handle and his outflung fingers caught the masonry of the door jamb. 'Peregrine might have warned me,' he thought in irritation, as he realized that there were two steps down into the body of the church, very close and unexpected, and that the interior was so badly lighted as to appear black dark to anyone going in from the brightness of the afternoon. He went down the steps with care, closing the door after him.

It was a very old, low-built church, with wide, semicircular arches on squat pillars of immense strength. The windows were of grey glass which had somehow survived from medieval times. It was full of striations and bubbles, and painted with the elaborate interlacing patterns in brownish black which are known as grisaille. The resulting gloom would have been much admired by lovers of the barbarism of the Gothic style.

Harry had to feel his way forward, edging through the box-pews which filled the nave like an attentive wooden congregation. At last he reached the space in front of the altar. Then he could see on one side of the chancel two recumbent alabaster effigies under an elaborately carved canopy. It made a separate tiny roof over them, shaped like a mass of stone icicles. Round the base were carved heraldic shields and kneeling down, Harry examined these and recognized one as the coat of arms which was displayed on the panels of the great travelling coach which had been sent to meet him. Standing again, he stood motionless for a long time, gazing at the beautifully-carved alabaster features of the husband and wife who were regarded as the founders of his race. He felt profoundly moved. The whole atmosphere of the place moved him, and the fact that his father's family, of whom until recently he had known nothing, could be traced back to these serene faces. He stood there as if in a trance and it was a long time before he felt the desire to look further.

Then he began to explore the church. His eyes had grown used to the light and he found a brass let into the floor, which was to the memory of another ancestor. Then he found wall tablets to others. None of the dates on the memorials were very recent and he remembered that he had heard something of a mausoleum, built in the grounds of Ramillies.

After going slowly round all the walls, Harry began to feel that he knew the cold, shadowy, ancient building. He returned to the alabaster effigies and traced with his finger the delicately indicated joinings of armour and folds of linen. It came to him that it was something to be the heir of the Akehams; it was indeed! There were honours and traditions which had been theirs, time out of mind. It seemed almost as though tradition could be felt and touched, here. The shields bearing heraldic devices which were as yet unfamiliar to him told him that the Akehams had married into other families who had also trailed long traditions, long habits of ruling and possessing, behind them. In the complete silence he realized that he owed these passive, calm figures something; a continuation. An upholding of honours.

At last Harry aroused himself somewhat from his reverie. Time must be passing – he had no idea how long he had spent in the church. Peregrine would long ago have reached home and all the mass of servants at Ramillies would be preparing dinner for him – for him, the Earl – all that care and work.

Yet it seemed different now, to Harry. He saw that he was not just one unassuming being. He was many men, stretching back into the mists of antiquity. He was a link in a chain. He was, in being the tenth Earl, an Office as well as a perishable human being. He was the life tenant of a position which would go on into the future as it had come out of the past.

He walked to a central point, in front of the altar. There he drew in a breath and raised his head proudly, gazing ahead and making a silent vow, to uphold the honour of his race. For five minutes he stood motionless, then he turned to walk slowly and thoughtfully down the aisle. As he approached the door into the outside world, he was beginning to feel ready to assume the rights and responsibilities which had become his.

Before he could reach out and open the door, it swung inward, pushed by some force from outside, and, with a smothered scream, Laetitia, Countess of Elmet, fell headlong into his arms.

CHAPTER FOUR

The Church

She was exceedingly wet.

That was Harry's first coherent idea, when he found – his arms having instinctively closed round her – that her arms were round his neck and a mass of soft curls was pressed into his face. Accordingly, he said so.

'You are exceedingly wet,' he remarked, removing his face from the curls and bending his neck so that he found himself looking down an inch or two at a straight little nose and eyelashes bearing drops of rain like dew.

'Who are you?' Laetitia withdrew herself from his arms and he helped her to stand firmly. She was trembling from the shock of the fall. 'You would be wet if you had been out in all this rain,' she added less indignantly. After all, he had saved her.

'Harry Akeham . . . at your service, madam. It was lucky that I was here to catch you. Is it raining again? I almost fell down those steps myself when I came in.' Too late, he realized that he had automatically given her his old name, just when he had been feeling so dedicated, so ready to take up his new one. His eyes were used to the light and he could see that she was very lovely and that her clothes were expensive.

'I had to take shelter.' Her voice was gentle and hesitant. 'I didn't think there would be anybody here. You won't tell them you've seen me, will you?'

'Of course I won't. Particularly as I don't know who they are, or who you are.' His voice was warm and protective.

'I'm running away. Do you think that is quite dreadful? I have been driven to it, you see.'

'I don't see, but come and sit down and tell me all about it. Is it raining so hard outside? When I arrived it was fine.'

Laetitia could not help deciding that he was a friend. It was in every tone of his voice, in the comforting clasp in which he had held her, in the considerate way in which she had been released and helped to stand alone, and in the way in which, as though it were the most ordinary thing in the world, this half-seen, complete stranger was offering to listen to her troubles. And then to start the topic of the weather, so that she could accept or reject his offered sympathy easily –

'You know what uncertain weather it has been,' she said tentatively.

'Yes. Bother Saint Swithin. Don't you long for fine, dry weather? It is weeks since we had twenty-four hours without rain. But I did think today would be better.' He had guided her into the nearest pew and they both sat down.

'It has come on to rain cats and dogs in the last half hour.'

'Why are you running away?' asked Harry.

The dark church, the unknown confidant, acted on Laetitia like a confessional.

'Because they want me to marry the Earl of the Ainsty.'

It was Harry's turn to be hesitant. At last, 'Don't you wish to marry him?' he said.

'My goodness no. Not at all. I don't want to marry, and he least of all.'

'Is he so very dreadful?' asked Harry meekly.

'I expect so. His cousin certainly was.'

'The ninth Earl?'

'Yes.'

'Did they want you to marry him too?'

'They tried to make me,' said Laetitia darkly.

'Surely it is simple enough to refuse?'

'You don't know my Aunt, Lady Langbar.'

'No, I have not that pleasure.'

'Or you wouldn't ask that question, you know,' explained Laetitia kindly. Harry wondered how anyone could browbeat this artless creature.

'Forgive my curiosity, but why should your terrifying Aunt be trying to force you to marry first one Earl and then another?'

'She tries to make me marry anyone who is rich and suitable and the Earls of the Ainsty are very rich and very suitable. The ninth Earl was unmarried and a most odious man.'

'I never met him.'

'He died and I wasn't a bit sorry,' said Laetitia with what for her was viciousness. Then she remembered something. 'Didn't you say your name was Akeham?'

'I did. My father was of a junior branch.'

'Then I have been very wrong to speak so of them to you. Please forgive me.'

'You are in trouble and I am most anxious to be of assistance in any way I can. The Akeham family, as a whole, are only recently known to me – there is nothing to forgive – it was only yesterday that I came to this part of the world for the first time.'

Laetitia wondered how it was that she was able to talk with such unusual freedom to the young man beside her. She was now used enough to the lack of light to see that he was dressed in neat but very ordinary clothes and might be a curate, a librarian or something of that kind. He was gazing abstractedly into the space ahead of him.

'Have you met the tenth Earl? My Uncle says he is a country clown, without breeding.'

'That is very bad. You can't be expected to marry such a person. Yes, I know him. We came up north together.'

'If someone loved him, they would not worry. If I loved anyone it would not be for . . .'

'You must forgive me if I do not understand quite why the Earl is regarded as so very suitable.'

'My estates march with his on his northern boundary, and I am poor, while he is rich.'

Harry thought that judging by her dress, her impoverishment was something very different to the poverty he knew, but went on, 'I see. Don't you think he might have something to say in the matter? He might be as unwilling for the match as you are.'

'The ninth Earl wasn't. He was bold, and . . . made advances . . . and . . .'

'And frightened you,' thought Harry, looking sideways at her and noticing the way she had shrunk into herself, her eyes looking big and terrified at the memory. Like a flower which responds to the sun by opening and the rain by closing, she would be wounded by a sharp word and withdraw all the delicate tendrils of sensitive response.

'Now you have run away from your cruel Aunt, where are you going to run to?' he asked in a conversational tone.

'I am going to find work under another name, and keep myself by my own efforts.'

'You must have been unhappy for a long time to come to this.'

'I have been,' she said simply.

They sat quietly for a while and Harry reflected that he could not possibly allow her to go unprotected into the world on this hare-brained scheme. An idea began to form, but he needed time to develop it.

'You seem to be rather unprepared for your adventure. That may lead you into all sorts of difficulties. Why, you are soaking wet. Suppose you come down with a chill in a strange place under a false name, with no one to care for you? What would you do?'

'I don't know.'

'How are you travelling?'

'My horse is tied up outside. I was getting on so well. I said I had a headache when Aunt and Bella were setting out in the carriage. Then I told my maid that I felt a good deal better and would follow them on horseback – they had gone to Malton to call on the Misses Godwin – and then I rode off. If it had not come on to rain I would soon have reached York, sold the horse and taken the stage out of the county.'

'You make it sound very simple. I don't think it would have gone quite like that . . . you would have been missed and traced in no time and brought back. Would not that have been worse?'

'It would. Much worse. Yet, at least I would have tried. Only I was becoming so wet and could hardly see my way, the rain was beating in my face so. When I saw this church I thought I would shelter until it was over. Perhaps the rain has stopped.' His words had wrought on her to such an extent that she was no longer so sure that she ought to go on; besides, she was really very wet.

'I have an idea – that is, if you are determined to leave the protection of your family and earn your own living.'

'It is what I want above all things.'

'You are hardly in a position to arrange it but I could look out for a suitable post with a respectable gentlewoman if you are in earnest.

Were you thinking of becoming a companion? Then – if I found you something – you could adventure with less risk. Though why a person like yourself, with estates and (as your Aunt is Lady Langbar) possibly some title of your own . . .'

'I am the Countess of Elmet,' admitted Laetitia.

'. . . why a countess should do such a thing, passes understanding.'

Then Laetitia talked for a while, as she had never been able to with anyone else, about her life since going as an orphan to Langbar Hall, until Harry no longer thought that it passed understanding, only that he himself would have run away long before. By the time she came to a halt he was only too ready to help her escape from it. His plan was maturing every minute.

'If I can find a suitable post for you –' she clasped her hands at that, and gave him a supplicating look from deep blue, innocent eyes '– how can I tell you of it? Would you be willing to return to Langbar Hall until it is arranged?' His voice was very gentle as he put that question, and as she considered it she shivered inside her wet clothes.

'I would wait . . . if it were not for too great a time . . .'

'As short a time as possible. At present I am living at Ramillies and you are at Langbar Hall. I'm not sure where that is.'

'If you are living at Ramillies it will be easy to meet and make arrangements. My Uncle is to call on the tenth Earl tomorrow. That is why I decided to run away today. He will be arranging to throw the Earl and me together; he is going to invite him to dinner next week. If I come to Ramillies or if you accompany the Earl to Langbar Hall there will be an opprotunity for me to speak with you.'

Harry asked curiously, 'Was it the idea of having to live in that great pile that prejudiced you so against Lord Ainsty?'

'In Ramillies?' she cried. 'Oh, no. I love it!'

'You love it?'

'You sound surprised – and yet you are living in the house?'

'I am.'

'But do you not find it the most beautiful place in the world?'

'Perhaps I have not yet grown to know it,' he said humbly.

'I have known it from childhood. To be in Ramillies is like living in a painting! Past Earls not only built a palace but so tamed nature that the surrounding hills and valleys are like a painting by

Claude. The sweeps of trees are just where they ought to be for the best effect. The river has been made to flow in the most picturesque way and under a bridge whose equal is only seen in dream. If a Lord Ainsty fancied that a height would be improved by being crowned by a pyramid, then it is so crowned!'

'You are eloquent,' said Harry. There was no stopping her.

'The mausoleum is considered a building of great beauty. It is disposed on an eminence and convinces the ungodly that death is a higher and more heavenly state. The Temple of Fortune – have you seen that yet?'

'No.'

'The Temple of Fortune might have been wafted from the Greece of Antiquity. Only so can it have achieved such perfection.' She paused for breath.

'Then could you not have married the ninth Earl for the delights of Ramillies?'

'No. There are more important things even than Ramillies. I could not marry for place or position.' Her voice stopped, the bubble of her enthusiasm was pricked, and Harry felt that if they talked longer she might begin to regret her openness. He rose and offered her his arm. Together they went back to the door of the church, up the two steps and into the air again.

The rain, sharp but short-lived, had stopped and the sun was showing a watery gleam. Laetitia's horse was cropping the grass contentedly and Harry's was in a corner of the churchyard.

'You will return to your Aunt's house?' he asked anxiously, having helped her into the saddle.

'Yes. If you are not too long in helping me to my escape.' She looked down, at once aloof and conspiratorial. 'If help does not come quickly I will take matters into my own hands again.'

The very thought of what she might do, of her innocence and helplessness, turned Harry's blood to water. 'Within a week, if at all possible,' he said hastily. 'They may not realize that you made the attempt today. It is important that they do not.'

'Be sure of it. I shall say I lost my way, took shelter from the rain and waited for it to stop. In its way that is true enough.'

'Very well.' He released her bridle and stood back as she trotted sedately through the open gate. Harry realized that when she entered she had been in too much of a hurry to close it behind her. It was as well that his own mount had not taken it into his head to wander off. The placid animal was still there, however, and in an hour he would be home. Home! The word had risen unbidden.

As he rode back, Harry had no difficulty in finding his way and he was eagerly on the lookout for the first signs of his inheritance. Laetitia's vision of it had entered Harry's mind and now he saw through her eyes, as the seductive charm of the landscape enfolded him.

Nor was Ramillies slow to welcome him. Signs of its approaching presence abounded, outflung with a generous hand. From every direction the traveller passed obelisks, romantic pillars, rustic fortifications and outworks in the grand manner. Vistas were prepared to open up before the wayfarer. The house itself, glowing golden like a cloud, shimmered briefly on the horizon, then was hidden by trees and revealed itself later, nearer, and from a different angle.

'It is like some home of faerie,' he thought after one such glimpse of his own distant frontage, all solid six-hundred and sixty feet of it, giving the illusion of being a floating mirage.

And so the Earl went home.

CHAPTER FIVE

The Plan

Harry found, on only his second awakening in his sumptuous bedroom at Ramillies, that already it was becoming familiar to him. Looking round, he recognized and liked the furnishings, and he liked the pleasant and helpful manservant who appeared so readily. His happy mood continued as, with his thoughts conjuring up visions of Hannah Clare sharing all this with him, he looked out of the windows and saw that it promised to be a fine day, walked downstairs and greeted the housekeeper, and finally found an excellent breakfast prepared for him in the small room where he had dined with Peregrine on the previous evening.

Immediately after breakfast the agent who dealt with the day-to-day running of the estate waited on him. Listening to his explanations of affairs, Harry realized that on the estate he could if he wished take a much more active part than his cottage visiting of the previous day.

It seemed that there were many paths open to him. Everyone he met had a different idea of how he ought to spend his time. From the least of his servants to the grandest of the acquaintances he made in the course of the following few weeks, they were all anxious to persuade him to go in the particular direction they considered best.

Harry found himself very ready to consider all their hints and suggestions, only reserving to himself the right to decide in the end what path he wished to follow – what kind of Earl he intended to be.

When the agent had gone, Harry went in search of Peregrine.

Since their after-dinner conversation of the previous evening, Harry knew his cousin much better, and liked him a good deal less. Yet he went in search of the older man with something like fascination.

They had shared dinner in the family dining-room and afterwards, over their glasses, Peregrine had allowed Harry to discover that he had been in his youth a dissolute rake-hell who had ruined his health and spent all the money he could get hold of in running a course of debauchery in London. He had offered himself as a guide to a nauseous underworld.

Yet this morning he found Peregrine in the library and in much the same negligent attitude as before, leaning against a bookcase with a book open in his hands.

'You surprise me, cousin, after our talk of last night. Your chief pleasure nowadays seems to be in scholarly and antiquarian books.'

'When the bodily appetites have been exercised to exhaustion, then one can turn to the pleasures of the mind.' Peregrine's dull eyes seemed to glitter as he added, 'They can be fully as strange – as exciting, as convoluted, as weird – as bodily pleasures, believe me.'

Harry put hearty friendliness into his voice as he answered, 'I shall explore the bookshelves with delight. I look forward to it.'

Peregrine's eyes dulled and dropped to his book as he answered, 'Other delights with our schoolmistress are in store for you today. Is she not coming to drink tea with we two bachelors?'

As though Hannah were to arrive any minute, Harry drifted over to the window which overlooked the steps up to the main entrance on the north front. The tall elegant form of Hannah Clare was nowhere to be seen – indeed, she was not expected until afternoon – but there were two mushrooms mounting the steps and being admitted by the butler to the dignities of Ramillies.

'Those are the Misses Godwin,' said Peregrine over Harry's shoulder. 'You must go and receive them, I think, milord.'

'Did you say they were connections of the family?'

'Yes. Distant. They take care to maintain the privileges of relationship. Were you not wanting more family?'

'Are you coming?' asked Harry, feeling momentary nervousness at formal entertaining.

Peregrine's smile was more sardonic than amused. 'I am never seen by visitors to the house. They do not interest me nor I them.'

The mushrooms turned out on closer acquaintance to be two small ladies in very large hats. They were sitting on the edge of the most uncomfortable chairs they could find in the great saloon, with their hands clasped in their laps, beaming comfortably at one another. Harry became quite calm. How can one be nervous with a small mushroom peeping out at one from under its hat and offering a mitten-clad and diminutive paw?

'You will excuse us calling so soon and in all our dirt,' said the spotlessly clean Miss Godwin. 'We walked across the park.' She extended a tiny foot in a stout brown half-boot for his inspection. He almost replied that mushrooms must be expected to have feet at least slightly marked by mould, but managed to restrain himself.

'These are our garden hats and not at all the thing for calling at Ramillies,' said the second sister, indicating her shady brim, 'but this is quite a family thing, no formality, and we must protect our complexions from the sun. We did so want to know how your father's son would look – the dear boy! So many years since we saw him!'

Harry's heart was now completely melted towards them.

'Did you know my father, madam?'

'He was the dearest child! He was here on a visit in – was it seventy-three, Sarah, or seventy-four?'

'Do you think me like him?' asked Harry, who was curious on this point.

'Oh, very like! He has dear Henry's nose and forehead, has he not, Martha?'

'But he has not the Akeham build, you know. You will forgive me mentioning that,' said the elder Miss Godwin, emboldened and warmed by Harry's smile. 'The Akeham men are usually six feet or over. Your eyes and teeth, though –'

'He has kind eyes, has he not, Sarah?'

'They are very fine, and I hope – we hope – that you will do us the honour of a call, dear boy. We do so hope that you will pop in and out just as if our home were your own.'

'Where do you live?' asked Harry, who would not have been

surprised to find that it was inside one of the fanciful buildings that decorated the park.

'In Malton. Such a convenience! All the shops very handy! And a mere six miles to stroll over to visit you, dear boy!'

'It sounds most convenient,' Harry had discovered that they tended to speak alternately, nodding at one another, and wearing their large hats (vastly elegant, though they had been referred to so deprecatingly) they were more enchanting than their down-to-earth selves could have realized.

'Maiden ladies such as ourselves have a great many worries, of course,' sighed Miss Martha.

'Can I help?'

'We would be glad of your advice! It is the paperhanging.'

Harry looked sympathetic.

'We are planning to hang wallpaper in the best bedroom. But who is to hang it, you know? There is Bill Johnson who will do it all in a rush and perhaps not well enough. And there is Francis Scott, who goes so slowly that we will have him for an age, and that will cost us so much in beer.'

'Have you bought your paper yet?' asked Harry.

'Oh yes. Bunches of roses tied with blue watered silk ribbon. Not real ribbon, you understand,' the elder Miss Godwin was anxious that there should be no misapprehension, 'but bearing the appearance of blue watered silk ribbon represented on the paper.'

'That will look very well.'

'It will, will it not? Lord Ainsty understands perfectly, the dear boy,' said Miss Martha Godwin to her sister. Before they could move on to consider the difficulties of making a paste which was thick enough but not too thick, another caller was announced and Harry rose quickly to greet the tall, slender man who entered the room.

'Your servant, sir; your servant, Miss Godwin, Miss Martha,' said Lord Langbar.

Harry met the frank appraisal of a pair of hooded grey eyes in a slender, aristocratic face. As he went forward he found himself wishing that he had indulged in new clothes. There was nothing of the dandy about Lord Langbar, but every line of his tall, imposing figure was immaculate, from the snowy cravat to the shining boots.

Lord Langbar, on his side, looking into the face of the younger man, was wondering how Crump could have seen the quick, vivid look and the eager intelligence in those eyes and put their owner down as a country booby. As Harry smiled and their hands clasped a wordless alliance was formed between them.

'Oh, your lordship, what a pleasure!' cried Miss Martha. 'It was only yesterday that we saw her ladyship and dear Isabella, and now to have the pleasure of meeting you. How is dear Lady Elmet's headache?'

'I was not aware that she had one,' replied his lordship. 'I was out on business most of yesterday. At breakfast this morning she appeared very much as usual.'

'I am so glad for the dear child,' said Miss Godwin. 'We were sorry to miss seeing her and gaining the benefit of her opinion on our wallpaper. Pray tell her, sir, that we are to place the pattern so that the bunches of roses come centrally over the chimney-piece, even though it does mean some awkward cutting near the door.'

'She will be interested to hear that,' replied Lord Langbar.

'Do you think, sir, that we ought to ask Bill Johnson, who is quick but careless, or Francis Scott, who is careful and takes an age, to hang it for us?'

'I rather gave the preference to the careful Francis,' put in Harry to Lord Langbar.

'Francis, to be sure. A good careful job is always the best in the long run.'

'He will cost more in beer,' explained Harry.

'It will be worth it,' considered his lordship.

'Then we will ask Francis Scott. What it is for us to have the advice of gentlemen! These undertakings can be very troublesome. I quite dread all the business of taking all the furniture out and then taking it all in again.'

'And there is the cost of the flour for the paste.'

'Perhaps you had better not have it done at all,' suggested Harry mischievously.

'Your lordship is teasing us! When we have bought the paper, you know!'

'We ought to be going, Sarah. Their lordships will be wanting to discuss politics and such like matters and Janey will be expecting our return.'

'Well, as to politics,' said Lord Langbar, stretching out his legs and making himself comfortable, 'you ladies are at this time as interested I think as the men. Can anyone talk of anything but the Queen's return? When I was in York yesterday I heard that they are getting up a Loyal Address to be presented to Her Majesty. I was glad of it. She should know of the support she has throughout the country.'

'The poor dear lady! We are glad to hear that something is being done!'

'She is being treated shamefully.'

'The whole country agrees with you, Miss Martha,' Harry's tone was serious. Not even the topic of Caroline of Brunswick-Wolfenbüttel would detain the Misses Godwin, however, when they had decided that they had stayed as long as custom permitted. They rose and made their way to the door, adding, 'We will leave you to discuss it . . . I remember when we were here last year at this time the early grapes were ripe . . . we will see you soon, we hope, Lord Ainsty. You must call, dear boy.'

'Do let me order a carriage,' he said, distressed at the idea of them walking so far. 'And if we have grapes, please permit me to give you some.' He was out of the room some minutes, finding that when the comfort and convenience of others was concerned, it came quite naturally to give the necessary orders. He was rewarded by overhearing a whispered comment of Miss Godwin's – 'so much more obliging than the ninth Earl, my dear!' – before he returned to the saloon and Lord Langbar.

'You have already met our mutual connections,' said that gentleman. 'The Misses Godwin are not slow to take advantage of relationship.'

'Are they related to both, sir?'

'Distantly. On their father's side to my family, on their mother's side to yours. It is the mainstay of their existence. They can be a welcome addition to society – do not despise them. Though I see you do not.'

'They seem worthy, good-natured souls.'

'And so they are.' The Misses Godwin having been thus disposed of, and a pause ensuing, Lord Langbar broke it with the remark, 'You will, I hope, join in the political life of the county. We need you keen young men. I don't need to ask your persuasion, I think. I can see that you have the right ideas. This whole business of the Queen is distressing.'

'I know that she has returned to the country.'

'Returned to be ignored by her loose-living, disreputable husband! No welcome, no home prepared for her. Had it not been for the action of Alderman Wood of London, she would have had to lodge in a common hotel. He gave her the use of his home and he and his family went to a hotel themselves. The whole country is distressed by her treatment.'

'She has been travelling for some time, has she not?'

'Driven out,' said Lord Langbar impressively. 'Now she has returned – the reigning Queen Consort – and to be treated so shabbily!'

For half an hour they chatted on political matters, getting on very well. Harry had not previously given such things much thought, and Lord Langbar took pleasure in explaining to him the way he ought to think on the topics of the day. Then he remarked, at a tangent, 'How fortunate you are in having your rooms facing south! It was considered a most surprising thing, I believe, when Ramillies was built. They are always excellently warm and sunny; very pleasant. I prefer it to our own east and west facing, though that too has its advantages. You will see for yourself when you visit us. Your grandfather, I remember, used to say that these rooms at Ramillies were positive ovens with very moderate fires.' Lord Langbar was convinced of the importance of the little things in life, as much as his connections the Misses Godwin. So that now the great topics of the day were disposed of, he went on to chat comfortably about his family, his heir's exploits at Oxford ('He thinks I don't know what he's getting up too, young devil') and about his daughter, Bella, who had made a conquest in her first season which was going to result in a fine match later in the year. 'You will meet Bella if you can dine next week, though Ughtred is at Oxford for another week or so. The younger girls do not come down to dinner, of course. But if you will please me by arriving early they would be permitted to come into the drawing-room for half an hour.'

'I would like that.'

'And then we have living with us our dear niece, Laetitia, who is the Countess of Elmet. A sweet girl.' Lord Langbar had taken care to discover before calling that the new Earl was unmarried. Having given him several opportunities to mention any affianced bride, he now dropped Laetitia into the conversation almost as an afterthought. Seeing Harry's look of interest, he told him something of Laetitia's background and her parents, referred casually to her estates, waxing confidential as he felt increasingly at ease with the new Earl.

'The only trouble is that she is so shy. That was why we did not find a match for her during the season. You have no idea how retiring she can be! If it had not been for her looks – she is something of a beauty – no one in Town would have noticed that she was there at all. When she is introduced to you as Lord Ainsty I doubt if you will get a peep out of her. One cannot be provoked by my late sister's child; her nature is so sweet. Yet if she will allow no eligible man to get to know her, she must want for a husband.' Lord Langbar felt at this that he had probably said enough. He had laid forth the bait and tried to avoid causes of misunderstanding. Things must take their course.

Harry had been listening and thinking and had at last made up his mind to take a risk.

'If through some – misunderstanding – she were to meet me and not realize that I am the Earl, would she be more at ease?'

'She would indeed. She can chatter away cheerfully enough when she is speaking to people of no importance.'

'As it happens, I think I have already met the Countess,' said Harry thoughtfully, looking at the carpet. 'I had not intended it to become public, because she did not realize who I am, and it would cause her embarrassment to have the mistake explained to her. She had taken shelter from the rain while out riding and I happened to be sheltering in the same spot.'

'Oh, indeed,' and Lord Langbar's eye lit up.

'You see that I have not yet bought any clothes suitable to my new position,' brought out Harry diffidently. 'And I must admit that I do not know the best tailors in this part of the country.'

'That is no problem,' was his new friend's prompt reply. 'Send your manservant over to talk to mine. You can find reasonable tailoring in York. Mine will give him the addresses and you will find very little time need be taken up by the matter.'

'That is most kind of you.'

'So Laetitia – deceived by your appearance, no doubt – did converse?' and Lord Langbar's eyes positively twinkled.

'Yes. It is a pity that when she knows who I am, at your dinner party, she will no doubt have nothing to say to me. I should have revealed my true identity at the time.'

'I wonder . . .'

'A cousin of mine is resident here, as librarian: Peregrine Akeham. Do you know him?'

'Peregrine Akeham! It is years since I heard of him. He used to be a sad rake, you know. I saw him racing a curricle through the streets of London and one met him in the gambling rooms. Until his father, the sixth Earl, died, that is. Since then he has been seen nowhere, by nobody. I did hear that he was kept up close here at Ramillies.'

'Might he accompany me when I pay my visit to you?'

Harry's eyes met those of Lord Langbar and there was no doubt that the ideas of both of them were following the same path, except that Lord Langbar's had leapt forward rather into possibilities which – because of the existence of a certain Hannah Clare – were not what Harry intended.

'You will not be able to have your new clothes made in time for next Wednesday, and if Peregrine were to enter the room a little before you –'

'Dressed very fine –'

'And my wife were to take him for you –'

'Lady Laetitia would think I was he –'

'We'll do it,' said Lord Langbar. 'My youth was full of such pranks. I will not enlighten my wife. No doubt we will suffer for it when we are found out, but what matter! Can you obtain Akeham's agreement?'

'I have no doubt of it.' Harry had realized that Peregrine had no morals at all, and was totally dependent on his own goodwill; and for the sake of helping Laetitia escape from unhappiness, he felt quite prepared to bend Peregrine to his wishes.

'We will make it a family party only. Soon enough you will have to meet the rest of the county – but they will quite understand if you do not wish to rush into it – everyone is well-disposed towards you. We will get our little prank over first, will we not. That will be the best thing.' Lord Langbar looked like a boy again at being a conspirator. After a pause, he went on, 'I can talk to you, Ainsty, and I have it in mind to tell you something few people know. My wife is a good creature, but she pushes Laetitia a little hard, and the girl is not altogether happy. There was an occasion when she was fourteen when she ran away and tried to hire herself out as a housemaid. Fortunately we found her in time otherwise who can tell what would have happened? Ever since then we have kept a strict watch over her and she has been docile. Because she will not stand up for herself she allows her feelings to prey upon her. My dear sister was just the same, though she was, I think, a bit more spirited than her daughter. They will both try to escape rather than have a confrontation.'

'It must have been very worrying for you.'

'Hmm! You can imagine. I tell you, because it would not be fair for you to be thrown together with her without knowing her history. You will treat this as confidential, I know.'

'Yes.' Harry realized uncomfortably that Lord Langbar was taking him as a serious suitor for Laetitia. If he explained that his interest was only friendly and protective – like that of an elder brother, perhaps – he would render himself ineffective. The false idea must be allowed to remain, even to be fostered. It seemed to be time to change the subject . . .

The plan for befriending Laetitia had started well, but for its further development Harry needed Peregrine's co-operation. Lord Langbar had told him that the sixth Earl was Peregrine's father by an irregular union, and that though his mother had tried to claim the succession for him on the death of his father, the marriage had not been valid. When he was left alone, Harry sat quietly for some time, thinking over Peregrine's character in the light of the facts as he now knew them and wondering what was the best method of approaching him to gain his co-operation. But before he had decided, the butler announced the last visitor of the day.

'Show Miss Clare in here, Bridges.' Harry wanted to see Hannah in this sumptuous setting, such a contrast to her humble schoolroom. He sent a footman to ask Peregrine to join them to preserve the proprieties, and ordered refreshments.

Hannah entered, giving the same impression of capable dignity. She seated herself when invited to do so and looked around with composure. Peregrine arrived, and they all conversed decorously over the tea-cups.

'Do you intend to use this room every day, my lord?' Hannah asked.

'I hardly know. My mother would determine such things, but she is not with me at present. You must advise me, Miss Clare. The whole garden side of the house is delightfully sunny and warm, and the view from the windows superb. You think that this room is not appropriate?' He noticed a slight unease in Hannah's manner. She glanced at the wall opposite and then away again.

'How can I presume to advise you? Yet you embolden me to say, Lord Ainsty, that this room is not meant for everyday use. Your housekeeper should cover the chairs – I'm sure they have gingham or holland covers – and likewise the curtains. And she should keep the blinds down. All the most expensive silks and exquisite furnishings are in here. The carpet is a very rare Aubusson. Sun will be harmful to them. When you are entertaining the county they can be uncovered and appear as fresh and new as ever, but if you use them like this for everyday they will soon be faded and worn, and what a pity that would be!' All this was said in such a melodious voice and Hannah looked so beautiful that Harry was charmed afresh.

'Holland or gingham covers it shall be. You have convinced me, Miss Clare. Admirable!' What a manager of all this she would make, he thought. Everything would run on oiled wheels. A load off my mind . . . would she have me? At least she would not be daunted by anything.

Harry would have gone on discussing household affairs had not a delicately stifled yawn from Peregrine made him change the subject. He asked after the school and was given a conscientious account of each small scholar. Harry tried hard to remember at least family names, hoping that he would soon know each child individually.

Hannah's calm on this occasion was almost unbroken and Harry might have wondered if he had imagined the fire beneath the ice if they had not touched on the subject of the return of Queen Caroline from abroad.

'Her treatment is monstrous,' declared Hannah, forgetting self-control for a moment and revealing passionate feeling.

'The whole country seems to think so. The King will not be

swayed, though, by public opinion. He is moving against her. He has put papers regarding her conduct before the House of Lords and a select committee is to consider them.'

'Surely a Queen should not be so humiliated!'

'Perhaps it depends on how that Queen has behaved,' put in Peregrine.

'We all know how he has behaved to her. The people of London are for her. Did you hear that a mob broke Lord Castlereagh's fan-lights the night she returned and since then they have broken thirty panes of glass in the Marquis of Anglesey's windows? Emotion is so fierce in her defence that the Life Guards are patrolling the streets of London to prevent more outbreaks of violence.'

'They do not approve of the past conduct of the King, but how will their violence help matters?' asked Peregrine, his eyes, cool and amused, watching Hannah's face. She had warmed into passion in her championship of the Queen.

'It is a matter on which I cannot help feeling strongly. When she first came over as a virgin bride he slighted her repeatedly because of – because of Mrs Fitzpatrick. Has he ever behaved decently to her? I am in sympathy with those who also feel strongly and are ready to demonstrate that fact. No doubt the noblemen can afford new panes of glass. The reigning Queen of our country cannot soon shrug off the insults loaded on her by that monster George the Fourth.'

Harry honoured her for her ardent championship of the Queen and was very ready to agree with her that the former Prince Regent must be a monster.

When Hannah had gone Harry asked, 'Did Miss Clare come up to the house at all during the time of the last Earl?'

Peregrine paused before replying and then he said, 'She did come.'

'Tell me what my cousin was like?'

Peregrine was quite ready to talk about the ninth Earl, in isolation. It was only when talk of the schoolmistress was combined with any mention of him that there was obvious withdrawal. Harry wondered again whether the ninth Earl had made advances to the dignified girl which she had resented. Had Peregrine taken her side? Harry hoped so.

'What was he like? There is a portrait on the wall behind you.' Harry turned round to look. There were several paintings on the walls of the room but only one was a formal portrait. It was a half-length, showing a young man, gun in hand, against a landscape background of Ramillies park. The house itself was shown two thirds of the way up the picture. One end of its frontage appeared behind the back of Joshua, ninth Earl, and a good deal of the other end of it seemed to protrude from his chest. In looks he was not like Harry, except that they were much of an age and both had dark hair with a hint of a wave in it. Joshua wore a high collar and had a bold eye and already the indications of a double chin. He had an aggressive air. If the finished portrait did not please him, one felt he might turn that gun on the artist. Truculent was the word that occurred to the schoolmaster in Harry. He could see how this man would have terrified Laetitia, Lady Elmet.

'He was a year older than you – not much of a scholar. He would have made a good soldier, I think. He was over six feet in height, as have been most of the Akeham men. You and I, my lord, are exceptions in being of a lower stature. The Bold Earl, I believe the servants called him. You could not be unaware of his presence even in a building the size of Ramillies.'

'Noisy?'

'Very noisy. He had – not to put too fine a point on it – a habit of shouting and banging about. By comparison you are likely to earn the name of the Quiet Earl.'

'Not only by comparison. I do love peace and calm. Silence has beauty.'

Harry stood for a time looking at the portrait.

'Not my idea of good *ton*,' added Peregrine. 'A gentleman of breeding should be able to combine excess with elegance.' His fastidious nose expressed his disdain.

The more Harry looked at the portrait the more he disliked the sitter. Joshua the ninth Earl appeared to be the type of man he would enjoy punching on the nose. It was not at all surprising to think that he had – Harry conjectured – been bullyingly lascivious in his manner towards Laetitia and, maybe, over-bearing with Hannah Clare. Was this portrait the reason for Hannah's uneasiness when she sat with them in the saloon? It was directly opposite her chair. If that was what made her uncomfortable he would receive her in future in another room.

It seemed a good time to ask Peregrine to play a part in the mistaken identity stratagem of the following Wednesday. The whole thing was rather difficult to explain, as Harry did not want to reveal his real motives in letting Laetitia and Lady Langbar think that he was the librarian, and the world-weary Peregrine was the earl.

'Ah, the lovely Laetitia!' he drawled when Harry had reached the end of what seemed to be a rather long explanation. 'You have an eye to her, my lord? And what of our schoolmistress, that ardent nature coated with ice?'

'I have the greatest admiration and respect for both Lady Elmet and Miss Clare,' replied Harry rather stiffly.

Peregrine gave his thin-lipped, sardonic smile and went up to prepare for dinner. Harry was left wondering just what the other man had been implying, and what thinking. Then decided that it did not matter. He planned to help Laetitia escape from her unhappy life and Peregrine's agreement to be mistaken for himself had taken the plan one step further. The day had been a trying one, with no one dear and familiar to share it; so he went to the small writing table in his dressing-room and began to write to his mother.

'Dear Mama, In your letter you accuse me of being an Imp of Silence – yet I have not been from home long, and much has been happening. There has scarcely been time to take up a pen. If only you had been with me! You could have shared it all and helped take off the strangeness of everything. That is not a reproach, dearest Mama. Your principles are sacred to me and I am not trying to change your mind. I said the days have been crowded. They have been momentous, for I believe that I have met the lady that I wish to marry. You will surely love her, for she is all amiability and goodness, and her capabilities are above those of most persons of either sex. Now, Mama, are you not just a little pleased at that? You often told me how you regretted the fact that our circumstances made it impossible for me to marry and bring you grandchildren to gladden your heart. In every respect Miss Clare is, I am sure, the very bride you would have chosen for me . . .' and for half a sheet Harry expounded the virtues of Hannah Clare as revealed in two brief meetings.

Then he went on to tell his mother about the Countess of Elmet. 'You would long to help her,' he wrote with absolute certainty of his mother's kindness and sympathy. 'And I beg that you will. She wants to escape from her overbearing Aunt and live peacefully. Will you let her believe that she is your paid companion on a short tour? It would give her time to decide what she really wants to do. She lost her mother-love so young. If you could have seen the poor child wet and distressed you would have taken her to your bosom in an instant. Can I persuade you to go with her to Scarborough? Then I could ride over to see you and she might, who knows, meet a suitable partner in life – the place has become very fashionable. Of course, you might prefer Bath, or Matlock, or a journey to the Lakes. The Countess mistook me for the librarian here and I have not enlightened her, so you can go on forgetting that I ever inherited . . .'

The household at Ramillies had had to live through many changes in the last year, and at first, although welcoming, they had been rather stiff and formal with Harry. For his part they had seemed only a mass of faces to him. But every day he knew them better. They were rapidly becoming individuals and he was learning how to sense the opinions which they did not express. On the whole, he realized that he himself was becoming popular with them, but there were people who were not.

On his way down the staircase to the small family dining-room where he was to dine with Peregrine, Harry caught sight of the housekeeper crossing the hall, and called out to her. She was a motherly woman and waited for him to speak to her with a gratified expression.

Without speaking Miss Clare's name, he mentioned her advice regarding the usage of the saloon. Mrs Gambol's face dropped. She was not deceived.

'That school teacher, was it, as put it into your head, milord? She puts herself forward a little too much, I'm thinking.' Harry inspired love, not fear, and Mrs Gambol risked being outspoken rather than see him take a wrong step.

'She does not put herself forward, Mrs Gambol. I asked for her opinion, and was pleased to receive such sound advice. You will shroud everything in gingham and whatnot and we will use the smaller rooms for everyday.'

Mrs Gambol sniffed, and her nose could express her opinions quite as well as Peregrine's expressed his.

'If it is *your* wish, milord . . .'

Harry smiled, amused at her little reservations, and Mrs Gambol's heart was won for ever.

There was one more thing he could do on this momentous day. When his manservant was putting him to bed, he could raise the question of new clothes. Lord Langbar's advice was to be taken. And that, though Harry did not realise it, was to make the manservant a very happy man.

CHAPTER SIX

The Dinner Party

Lord Langbar did not confide to his lady that Laetitia was to be led to believe that Harry was the librarian and not the tenth Earl. The difficulties of explaining it to her when at last it came out – as it must do eventually – came over him as he rode back from Ramillies. Away from Harry's presence he rather wondered how he had come to agree to it at all.

'Does he have to bring the librarian with him?' exclaimed Lady Langbar. They were sitting in the drawing-room, with its view over the shrubbery, at the time. 'Does that not show lack of taste, Langbar? A leaning towards low connections? Surely he should now shake off such ideas and associate only with people of his new station.'

'The librarian is a cousin, you recollect, my dear. Not recognized, of course –' he cleared his throat and looked over hastily at the group of girls sitting with their sewing '– but related, none the less. I think the new Earl is intending to be of benefit to his relative. He is certainly honouring him with his friendship.'

'Then I suppose we must make the best of it. You seem to have formed a high opinion of his sense and his person.'

'I took a liking –' Then, suddenly remembering that it was Peregrine who would be appearing as the Earl, he added, 'The librarian, too, is a most worthy young man. If Ainsty takes him up, you know . . .' He left a significant pause and his wife nodded gravely.

Among the group of Langbar daughters, their cousin Laetitia had been listening intently to this conversation and was elated. Harry Akeham was coming to dine. She could not remember anyone from whom she had felt such understanding. Finding a friend was such a rare event to Laetitia that it overshadowed her fear of meeting the new Earl of the Ainsty. All the uncomfortable feelings aroused by that event could be forgotten as she looked forward to meeting Harry and hearing his plan for her new life.

In the few days which elapsed between Lord Langbar's visit to Ramillies and the Earl's arrival to dine at Langbar Hall, Lady Langbar was surprised at Laetitia's docility. From previous experience she had expected her to be unwilling to take an interest in what to wear and to appear distressed at her Aunt's well-meant advice on how to captivate the male sex.

This time, she showed a very proper interest in her gown, which had a high body and was tight to the shape and very much decorated round a fairly wide hem. She seemed also to like the accompanying slippers of white satin and the white kid gloves, and to be concerned about her hair. This was to be dressed in the French style, in a profusion of curls low at the sides of her face hiding her forehead, the hind hair brought up onto the crown of the head and partly concealed by a garland of roses placed very far back.

True, she stood gazing into space when her Aunt lectured her, but this was a decided advance on a frightened expression which always had the effect of stimulating Lady Langbar to attack. The only fear troubling the Aunt was that this docility might be due to some plan to run away before the dinner party took place and she kept a sharp watch to make sure that there was no opportunity for that.

Harry had worked and worried in the interval. His first letter to his mother had not been enough to settle everything, but in the end he had prevailed.

The fact was that Mollie, once her beloved son was away from her for the first time in his life, had felt very lonely and missed him very much. After only a few days she regretted taking such a firm stand over his inheritance. Not that she was willing to accept it and all that it entailed, oh no! But she need not have been so very positive! She could have left a little room for manoeuvre! This thought came to her whenever she was not on guard to prevent it.

When Harry's first letter arrived she was at first outraged by his suggestion that she take part in duplicity, for his plan for Laetitia could only be regarded in that light. Time and reflection won her over a little. Scarborough had always had attractions for her. Accounts of it had raised a desire to visit the town. She had not acknowledged these longings, for Mollie did not believe in wasting time wanting things which she could not have.

Accepting Harry's offer of a holiday in Scarborough (for she did not want to go to any of the other places he mentioned) would not be condoning his new role in life, exactly, she argued with herself. She would be near to him without capitulating by going to stay at Ramillies. He would ride over to see her and she could satisfy herself that he was well, without being committed to further concessions.

Yet she did not wish to visit Scarborough alone.

Who was there to accompany her? Her uncle at the vicarage was in poor health and could not travel, and his daughter Mary was busy looking after him. In her small circle of friends there was no one who was at liberty to go with her.

It was ridiculous, of course, for anyone placed as Laetitia was to want to run away from home and accept such a lowering of caste, but young women often had ridiculous impulses and fancied themselves ill-used. She could see that to live incognito with herself would be a quite unexceptional way for Laetitia to come to her senses and realize how well off she was at home at Langbar Hall.

At last Mollie wrote to Harry agreeing completely to his plan. Laetitia was to have the post of paid companion, paid by Harry in fact but through her, and they were to go to Scarborough together. She was to be kind to the girl and in return Harry was to visit them and bring for her inspection the young woman he wanted to marry.

It was at that point that Mollie's motherly feelings were most nearly involved, and even in her innermost thoughts she evaded dwelling on it. Harry told her that she would find the girl all she could wish for him. How difficult that was, he had no way of knowing.

How sublimely confident he was of her approval! How little prepared she was to give it! How ready to hate any chit of a girl who presumed to think herself good enough for Harry!

In the case of Laetitia whom he only wanted to help, she was prepared to regard him as a good judge of the case; but when it came to Hannah Clare her opinion of his capabilities plummeted.

How could he possibly decide on the right person to marry? It was much too vital, too important a decision for a young man to make. He had too little experience! Would be taken in by any wiles which might be thrown at him! Would drop to any lure, be decoyed by any transparent subterfuge! It was unfortunate, thought Mollie, that no woman existed who was good enough for Harry.

She made her preparations to go to Scarborough.

Harry had taken Lord Langbar's advice about clothes, and as well as what appeared to be an abundance of clothes for himself, a new coat and pantaloons had been ordered for Peregrine. At Lord Ainsty's request, Mr Akeham's clothes were given first priority, so that on the day of the dinner party he was able to wear them and look most distinctive. He had a kind of negligent grace, an air enhanced by the slanting silvery scar. Peregrine drove the light barouche and they did not take any servants with them. They were shown into the drawing-room together, with Harry hanging back slightly as the butler announced their names. Lady Langbar went forward in the most natural manner to Peregrine, bestowing as she went a gracious nod on Harry, and no one explained her mistake to her.

With the exception of the heir, all the Langbar children were gathered in the drawing-room to meet the guests. They made a pleasing picture, for they were all well dressed, graceful and healthy.

At first Harry hardly recognized Laetitia in her evening clothes. She was standing beside Bella. Then she caught his eye and they exchanged a look, before Lady Langbar pulled her forward to introduce her to Peregrine.

Watching Lady Langbar's simper, Laetitia's one terrified glance at Peregrine, then her dropped eyes and rigid lips, Harry felt once again all the urgent desire to help her and to protect her which had moved him in the church.

The short time before dinner passed in meeting the children,who produced their drawings and albums to entertain the visitors. Then they were sent off to the nursery, and, 'Lord Ainsty, will you take in my niece Laetitia . . . Mr Akeham, if you will be so good . . .' Harry saw Laetitia's hand tremble as she laid it on Peregrine's arm and hoped that it would not be too long before he had an opportunity of reassuring her that an escape was within reach. He was within sight of her at the dinner table, near enough to exchange an innocuous sentence or two, and she seemed to draw support from the little contact they had.

It could be seen quite quickly that Lady Langbar was not a monster. But how little sympathy there was between her personality and Laetitia's! The dominating, capable woman and the gentle clinging girl could not help but irritate one another. Harry wondered how Laetitia would manage if she had to run a household. Badly, he feared! He could see her making a suitable bride for a man who only wanted a sweet and decorative wife. Perhaps she would find such a one in Scarborough, of suitable rank. Harry mentally compared Laetitia with Hannah Clare and Laetitia came off badly in the comparison. Hannah would never run away to evade difficulties, of that he was sure.

On the whole, Harry in his inconspicuous role of librarian enjoyed the meal. Eating good food in surroundings where everything spoke of wealth and ease, and where there was a sweep of fine countryside outside the windows, this could only be pleasant. The rest of the company talked of things which interested him – books, politics, painting – with elegance of manner. He wished that he could have entered his new life gently, with a spell of such obscurity, becoming used by degrees to society – instead of being plunged at once into the limelight of the centre stage.

At the end of the meal, Peregrine, after a glance at Harry, agreed to Lord Langbar's suggestion that they forego their port and move with the ladies out of the house to take coffee on the grass, under the spreading shade of a cedar.

The whole party stood around in the warmth of the summer evening, chatting over their coffee cups. Lady Langbar's coffee was always particularly good. Harry found himself revelling in the tiny coffee can of fine china, the fragrant fluid, the luxury of idly consuming it in these outdoor surroundings. His part as the presumed librarian gave him a double pleasure; because he was a little apart, he was observer as well as actor in this play.

At last Lady Langbar suggested that the young people might like to explore the grounds. While they could not be compared to Ramillies, she remarked to Peregrine, she hoped they might find them not unworthy of notice. There was a summerhouse in the shape of a temple, a shrubbery with gravel walks, the wide sweep of shorn grass reaching to the Ha-ha, and the flow of the park with its deer and cattle beyond that.

'The shrubbery, I think,' said Bella brightly to Harry. 'May I have your arm, Mr Akeham? Letty, I will leave Lord Ainsty to you.' So they set off in that order, leaving Lord and Lady Langbar under the cedar tree, at liberty to debate their characters; at liberty for Lady Langbar to express her disappointment that Lord Ainsty was far older than she had been led to expect, and she did not know that she liked him, but that Letty had really borne up much better than usual.

The arrangement of pairs – Peregrine and Laetitia following Harry and Bella – soon gave way to a more satisfactory arrangement. Laetitia was uneasy in the company of the supposed tenth Earl and Harry found that he had little in common with Bella. They stood in a group to examine a sundial in the centre of a grass plat, and it was with general relief that when they moved off again Peregrine started with Bella and left Laetitia to follow with Harry. When the first two vanished round a bend in one of the shrubbery walks, Harry and Laetitia were able to drop back and pace slowly along a gravel walk in the shelter of a high hedge of beech. Ahead of them they could hear Bella's bright flow of chatter and the amused tones of Peregrine's voice.

'Do you have any news for me?' asked Laetitia, as soon as they were sure of not being overheard.

'Yes. It is all right.' Those words were enough to relieve her anxiety. The tone of reassurance reached her. She wondered why she felt so comforted by his presence, yet did not question the fact that she knew she could unhesitatingly claim his protection and that he would always give it.

'Lord Ainsty,' Harry went on, 'is kindly anxious to be of benefit to me and mine. He has suggested that my mother spends some time nearer to us. She is to come to Scarborough, she cannot do so alone, so is looking for a companion. Paid,' he added quickly. 'She was going to advertise for a suitable person, but I suggested a Miss Elmet as being ideal.'

'Miss Elmet,' said Laetitia, taking his arm, leaning on it, and looking happy. 'Yes, I am sure Miss Elmet will do her best to please.'

'Are you going to tell your Aunt and Uncle?'

'Oh, no! They would never permit it. When is Miss Elmet to take up her post? Tell me. I will be there. Uncle and Aunt will know nothing about it,' she added with satisfaction.

Harry mentioned the day and time. She was to meet Mrs Akeham in York and they would travel to Scarborough together. Lord and Lady Langbar would never suspect her of going to Scarborough, so near at hand. If she were pursued, it would surely be in the direction of London?

'Yes. They would expect me to go there. I have other relatives – more distant – and on one occasion set off to go to them. However, they do not want the responsibility of having me . . . I could go to my own estates but they would find me there in no time. I am of age; if I could be firm enough I could insist on living there, but over the last few years everything has become run down and out of repair.' Her voice took on a note of quiet despair and Harry could not bear it. He recalled her thoughts into happier channels.

'It will give my mother such pleasure to have your company,' he told her. 'She has longed for a daughter. In fact I once had a baby sister, who died before I was old enough to remember her.'

'I am longing to meet Mrs Akeham! I'm sure that she will be kind and I will be happy.'

'The George, in Coney Street, York, on the fifth, don't forget,' he said hastily as Peregrine and Bella came into sight again and it looked as though the *tête-à-tête* were over.

Although Laetitia was content that Lord and Lady Langbar should be in ignorance of her whereabouts, Harry was not. At last, when he and Peregrine had said goodnight to the ladies and Lord Langbar walked out with them to the barouche, he was able to take him aside. Peregrine climbed up to sit and wait for him in the vehicle. Lords Langbar and Ainsty walked together in the silvery moonlight.

'I did not really approve of your plan. Yet it has worked admirably. I was pleased to see my niece talking to you so naturally.'

'My plan has – so to speak – extended itself,' admitted Harry. 'Your niece has, as you yourself told me, a great desire to try her hand at living in the world – not an easy thing for a high-born young woman. My mother is coming to spend some weeks in Scarborough, and I have suggested that Lady Elmet might reside with her for a while.'

'That seems an excellent idea,' said Lord Langbar, who in that instant saw his niece becoming Countess of the Ainsty in the very near future.

'Only – I hope I will have your forbearance so far, Lord Langbar – she is under the impression that she is to run away to be a paid companion to Mrs Akeham, and it is all to be quite unknown to you. Lady Elmet intends to be incognito. But I could not be happy if you did not know where your niece was. If you will agree to this, she will be under my mother's protection, and not many miles away. I don't see that she can come to any harm.' There was a long pause, while Lord Langbar said nothing and Harry felt sure that he would not agree, so he went on, 'If you feel you must, Lord Langbar, then you must reveal it all. Lady Elmet would withdraw her friendship from me in that case. I beg of you to allow her this escapade, as she thinks it.'

'Why not?' His lordship's tone was expansive. 'After she is safely away I will tell my wife that I have given my permission for her to visit your mother. The deception can hardly continue much longer. She will know soon who you are. Then, if she ever finds out that we know her whereabouts, she would probably think that they had only just been discovered to us.'

'That might well be her assumption, sir.'

'I look forward to meeting your mother, Ainsty. You must not keep her under a bushel.'

'No, indeed! I hope to persuade her to come and live at Ramillies with me. Your niece's presence will help in that, I am sure. She spoke to me with much enthusiasm of the house and its grounds. If she speaks so to my mother, she will feel the desire to see it. Once at Ramillies I have high hopes of her staying in the country.'

'It is good that a son has a proper value for his mother's company. I only hope that when our turn comes to be alone, Lady Langbar or I – whichever it may be – will be so much in request, by our children.' The older man was so serious and thoughtful that Harry grew almost embarrassed.

'You see, Mother and I only had one another . . .'

Shortly after the two men said goodbye, Harry climbed into the barouche next to Peregrine and they set off on their return journey under the light of the moon.

The household at Ramillies had by now taken Harry to their

hearts. They were anxious about his well-being, having not liked the ninth Earl and living in fear in case anything should happen to Harry and they should be faced with Peregrine as the eleventh – for there were very few males left now in the Akeham line, and if he were the only claimant, they thought that he might succeed in inheriting. They had not liked this informal arrangement at all. Carriages could so easily be overturned. They were all in a worry. What they would have done, had they known that on that evening Peregrine was being taken for the Earl and Harry for the librarian, is best left to the imagination. As it was, the housekeeper and the butler were keeping vigil one on either side of the door, and the house-steward was lying sleepless in his bed. One and all they were deciding to hedge Harry about in future with as many retainers as they could.

Laetitia could not hide her elation over the next few days. Although she had shown no interest in the pretended Lord Ainsty on the evening of the dinner, and had even been heard to say that she abominated him, her Aunt could indulge in self-deception as easily as less exalted mortals. She thought Peregrine was Lord Ainsty; she thought Laetitia ought to marry the holder of that title. Therefore, naturally enough, she saw Laetitia's light-hearted mood as confirmation of an attraction and forgot any impressions she might have had to the contrary.

Meanwhile Lord Langbar, who was nearer to the truth of the matter, kept a weather eye on his ward. He detected her ruse to escape almost as soon as she had formed it and helped her by every means in his power, mainly by keeping Lady Langbar out of the way at the crucial time. He had already sent one of his servants ahead on the morning of the fifth to call at the George in Coney Street, to make sure that a Mrs Akeham was staying there and find out what he could about her. This servant was loitering near the entrance to the George when Laetitia arrived and managed to avoid her seeing him by slipping behind a pillar. Having already found out from one of the maids at the inn that Mrs Akeham was a very nice, considerate lady who had booked two seats on the Scarborough coach, he returned to Lord Langbar to set that gentleman's mind at rest.

* * *

'Laetitia is missing!' exclaimed Lady Langbar dramatically.

'I know, my dear. In fact I have given her my permission to pay a visit.'

'What? To whom?'

'To Lord Ainsty's mother.'

Then, on his lady turning to give him a questioning look and remaining silent in suprise, Lord Langbar had the unenviable task of explaining what had happened. Apart from one or two involuntary exclamations, she was silent until the end. Then she placed a few sharp questions. Then, pacing to the window in a state of excitement, she took hold of the curtain and dropped it again, before turning to face her husband.

'We've got him,' she exclaimed triumphantly.

'What do you mean, my dear?'

'We've got him. He can't refuse to marry her now. After all this! No! She will be the Countess of the Ainsty this year. I will go farther. She will be his wife in under three months.'

CHAPTER SEVEN

The Escape

There was all the difference in the world between running off on the spur of the moment and making a premeditated escape; and Laetitia had wondered if she would have boldness and decision enough to carry it out. It was only her trust in Harry which made it at all possible. That was rash when she knew so little of him. But there are things which are not gauged by the formal introductions and the measured approaches beloved of society. When two personalities touch, it is a wonderful thing to feel the contact reverberating through to one's fingertips. Enough is known . . .

A portmanteau was out of the question. Without a qualm she left behind all her dainty things, her ivory-backed hairbrushes and silver-mounted flasks of scented waters. At the back of a drawer she found an old simple toilet set which she had used in her childhood and she touched it again with pleasure. Then she rolled it up inside two night rails and three lacy nightcaps. She chose the simplest of her clothing, and thanked her stars that young gentlewomen, whatever their rank, dressed very much alike during the better part of the day. A couple of round gowns of muslin, a plain silk dress to serve for all grander occasions, one warm shawl. A stout pair of half-boots in which she could both ride and walk and several pairs of soft slippers found their way into the bundle which she made and then wrapped overall in a warm travelling rug.

This bundle she hid in some bushes near the back entrance to the park, without being observed as she thought. The auguries were good. She would be able to enjoy the simple life for which she longed.

Early on the morning of the fifth, Laetitia, saying that she meant to ride before breakfast, had her dark bay mare brought out of the stables. Lady was a pretty creature, fifteen hands high with a small star on her forehead. It had been surprisingly easy to avoid Lady Langbar. Laetitia paused to retrieve her bundle and tie it to her saddle, then set off to ride to York and take up her post as Miss Elmet.

To go along the turnpike road would be to court disaster, for she would be remarked and remembered at every gate. Being a solitary traveller she could avoid it. For miles around Langbar Hall she knew the land well and could travel cross-country, picking her way round woods and across fields, down lanes and along bridle paths.

She had to skirt the outposts of Ramillies and did so warily, feeling much relief when she was past. Gradually she left behind the pretty undulating countryside and came into the flatter environs of York. Ahead, solidified greyness on the horizon, was the Minster, and as she worked her way towards it, the massive pile was sometimes hidden by a clump of trees or a farmer's barn, but always as the obstacles were passed it reappeared that much larger.

Soon she could distinguish the crocketted finials atop the towers and the glitter of the great east window. The Minster rose up behind the walls of the city as Laetitia approached by way of Monk Bar. The Bar itself was behind a clutter of small houses and shops, so that the composite picture before her was artistically composed into foreground, middle distance and background.

The foreground was the daily clutter of carts, people, carriages, baskets, driven cattle, children, all moving and living and having their being around the entrance to the city, or trying to crowd through the narrow stone gateway. The middle ground of the picture was the great medieval gateway itself, battlemented, flanked by walls, speaking of ancient grandeur. Then the background – the soaring cathedral with its reminder of eternal things. Laetitia longed to tilt back her head and drink in its timeless beauty against the sky, but it took all her nerve and all her presence of mind to guide her horse through the growing press of people and traffic. It was as well for Laetitia that Lady was a calm, placid creature, and that she was used to controlling her.

Goodramgate was a maelstrom, without an inch to spare, and High Petergate, Lop Lane and Blake Street were not much better. Before she reached the narrow congestion of Coney Street she had to pass Benson's stables and she turned in there to leave her mount.

'She may be here some weeks,' said Laetitia, handing over the reins. Lady wickered and swung her switch tail.

'She'll be all right, ma'am, right as if she were at home,' J. Benson reassured her. 'Excellent hay and corn at moderate prices.'

Who knew when she would be able to claim Lady again? Companions did not keep horses . . . carrying her bundle and with her nerves almost failing her now that she had to jostle her way on foot, Laetitia turned into Coney Street, made way for the Newcastle High Flyer Coach which was just leaving the Black Swan with all the stir and importance possible, and arrived at the door of the George preparing to ask for Mrs Akeham, with her throat suddenly dry and her voice vanishing within her.

Although she had been rooted for more than twenty years in one place, Mollie Akeham had not forgotten the lessons learnt when she was travelling on campaign. She had set her house in order and farmed out the care of her hens and flowers. Then, with the old travelling trunk which had seen such service, she had set out for the north. After the experience of travelling with an army, moving northwards through England by post was a positively luxurious experience. As they swept into York the bustle reminded her pleasantly of London or Brussels and she was very well satisfied with her accommodation at the George.

On the morning of the fifth of July she had woken early and set out to explore her surroundings. The chambermaid had commended the New Walk, so Mollie had chosen it for her object and walked from one end of it to the other and back before breakfast. Stretching from Ouse Bridge for a mile away out of the city, the Walk was some twenty yards wide, with the broad, busy river Ouse on the right and full-grown trees in all their beauty on the left. At that time in the morning Mollie had it almost to herself, but later in the day it would be full of fashionable people. On her return to the George, breakfast was being served and once that was over Mollie began hourly to expect the arrival of the girl who was to be her companion.

Then, if Laetitia were nervous, Mollie was not much less so. To be travelling, quite at leisure and with an ample supply of money (for, in accepting Harry's scheme, she had had also to accept the means of accomplishing it), on an expedition in pursuit of nothing but pleasure! How strange that was! Now she had time on her hands to think about it. To be in hourly expectation of a young woman of noble birth who wished to take the humble post of companion! To have to sustain goodness knows how many deceptions when all her instincts were for openness and honesty!

From his knowledge of her, Harry would have expected his mother to be longing for home at this point. But human beings who have lived in the same house for decades and love one another dearly can be as unknown to one another as though they lived at opposite ends of the earth. Mollie felt uncomfortable and nervous as she waited in the sitting-room at the George, but she did not in the least wish to be back at home. When Miss Elmet was announced, Mollie stood up and went forward eagerly.

She saw a girl of perhaps twenty-two years, though looking younger, in front of her. She was slender and beautiful, with her fair skin, soft golden hair and wide blue eyes, and very well dressed. So elegantly dressed, though in very simple clothes, that Mollie was taken aback. Then she saw the girl's gentle, modest expression and the shy way in which she seemed to hesitate to step further into the room – and Mollie's heart went out to her.

Crossing the floor quickly, she took the girl's hands in both her own and bent forward to kiss her cheek.

'Well met, my dear! So you are Miss Elmet! My son has told me of you.'

'I hope I will suit, ma'am,' said the Countess of Elmet.

'Very well, I do believe. Come over to this sofa. Do sit. Are you very tired? Do you want to remove your hat?'

Mollie drew the girl into the room and sat beside her.

Laetitia laughed tremulously. 'Madam, never was a companion met with such kindness.'

Mollie did not know what to say. She patted the hand she had taken in her own. 'I am hoping that you will be more like a friend or a daughter to me than like a paid companion. I have no daughter, not even a niece.' Finding that Laetitia was smiling but apparently wordless, Mollie decided to chatter on, to put her at her ease. 'I have bought seats on the coach for our journey to Scarborough tomorrow.'

'Oh, not until tomorrow, madam?' in a note of alarm.

'Why, no. Today's coach had already left York. There are two coaches each day in the season, I find. The Prince Blucher Post Coach sets off from the George here every morning at a quarter past nine and the Old True Blue from the Black Swan at nine o' the clock. There is little in it, you see. I daresay they vie with one another all along the road to see who can get there first. The Prince Blucher is billed as arriving at the Plough Inn, Scarborough, at four in the afternoon, in ample time to dine there. The Old True Blue sets down its passengers at either the Bell or the Bull. As we are staying at the George it seemed best to use the Prince Blucher so I have purchased two inside seats on it.'

'That seems the best plan,' agreed Laetitia, relieved that she would only have to step out of the door and directly into the coach. After all, it would not occur to anyone that she would spend a night in York and then go on to Scarborough. It was the last thing anyone in pursuit of her would expect! The best place to hide a leaf is in a wood and she now saw that the best place to hide a Yorkshire woman is in Yorkshire. Her own inclinations a fortnight ago would have taken her fleeing down the Great North Road to London where she would have been as conspicuous as a currant in a bun.

'I am not sure whether to approve of this city or not,' remarked Mollie, seeing that nothing but time would help Laetitia overcome her state of nervous agitation. 'In one respect at least it has my wholehearted support. The city is sending a Loyal Address to the Queen.'

'Oh yes, poor lady!'

'The whole affair is quite dreadful. The King has treated her abominably since she came back. Now he has laid certain papers before the House of Lords relating to Her Majesty's conduct while abroad, as I'm sure you know. A select committee is to consider them. How can George the Fourth, himself a monster of depravity, who has driven her to despair with his behaviour, now behave so to the poor creature he has wronged? Publicly to accuse her, the Queen of England! It is enough to put marriage itself into question when such things occur. And the loyalty of the country towards the monarchy is under strain.' Mollie spoke more heatedly than was her habit. Every woman in England would have been with her in this sisterly concern. If a Queen could be treated so badly, it augured worse for their own welfare in their minor spheres.

Mollie paused, then went on, 'Her Majesty has been a model of family behaviour. She went to see the statue of George III erected in her absence. Of course, she has that dual loyalty to him, being both his niece and his daughter-in-law. The action moved the populace to emotion and they pulled her carriage instead of the horses. Crowds of ladies were waiting there to greet her.'

'Indeed, madam? I had not heard of that.'

'And as for her husband! You will know that at both his Drawing Room and his Levée the Duchess of Gloucester presided, instead of Her Majesty, his lawful wife.'

Laetitia was recovering a little and, feeling it incumbent upon her to speak, said, 'I heard that both were very thinly attended.'

'Society is showing its opinion. I am delighted.'

'York's Loyal Address to Her Majesty is now being taken to London, I understand.'

'Yes, by one of your MPs – what do ye call 'em –'

'Marmaduke Wyville is taking it I think, though it could be Robert Chaloner.'

'Wyville,' Mollie patted Laetitia's hand again. 'That is the man, I'm certain of it.'

Gaining courage, Laetitia put a question. 'When you spoke earlier of York, you did not seem absolutely to approve of the city, ma'am?'

'The New Walk is elegant. I strolled there this morning. Otherwise it is a city with the worst set of streets I ever saw. These great overhanging houses! I declare the fourth and fifth storeys almost touch across the street and most of the streets seem to be like that. This one, Coney Street, could do with being a good deal wider with all the coaches to and fro every day. It is amazing no one is killed. I do not consider these overhangs healthy . . . there is barely a foot separating the upper floors of houses on opposite sides of the street. Sun and air are kept out and smoke is kept in.'

'The city has many beauties,' defended Laetitia. She was calmer now and Mollie's quiet voice did not intimidate her. Neither could she help liking someone who looked at her with eyes so much like Harry's, and with a smile reminiscent of his.

'Why, so I hear. And that is why I wish to see them. I would be sorry to leave the place without seeing its better side.'

Laetitia was in a quandary. She dreaded being discovered, being torn from her new protectress and marched back ignominiously to

Langbar Hall. To walk about the streets would fill her with nervous dread. Yet she had become a paid companion and must work to please Mollie.

'I will take you to see St Mary's Abbey,' she volunteered. 'It has a beautiful range of eight Gothic windows which are backed by elms, creating a charming scene of antique ruins. You will like it, I am sure.'

'And the Minster?'

'They are but a step apart. You will revel in the magnificence of our great church.'

'Could we spend the afternoon seeing these two places, do you think?'

Laetitia was carried away, as she had been when describing Ramillies to Harry. 'An afternoon is scarcely long enough to do them justice, or to exhaust one's delight in their beauties.'

Mollie listened and had an almost childish air of anticipation, so that for a moment Laetitia felt the older of the two. She smiled. Such open pleasure struck a chord in her own nature.

The two women spent the rest of the day very happily. When they returned to the George to dine they felt calmed and refreshed by contemplating tranquil beauty and spiritual grandeur. Laetitia had fortunately not met anyone she knew.

They dined alone in a private parlour, well pleased with one another, then retired early. They were aware that to breakfast in York and dine in Scarborough on the following day would be exhausting enough.

Their route was along the Turnpike Road. Laetitia leaned back in her corner in case anyone saw her when they stopped. During the course of the day they were to rattle through Ayton Gate, Scagglethorpe Gate with its weighing engine, Hartford Bridge Gate, Plaxton Gate, Huntington Gate and Hutton Gate, after setting off in fine style through Monkbridge and Spittle House. The main source of enlivenment on the journey was the coachman's efforts to keep the Old True Blue in sight.

The route went close to Ramillies and when they neared it, Mollie asked if it could be seen from the road. Laetitia thought so, and Mollie looked out earnestly. She was enchanted by the rolling patchwork of the countryside and declared it as comely a scene as she had ever travelled through. Then she glimpsed the fantastic outline of Ramillies against the sky. The sight quietened her. She had not really believed in the place! But that dome and spiky outline of roofs must be large indeed to be seen so far away and even at this distance to look impressive.

Until they were quite near Scarborough their fellow passengers were nothing remarkable. Then an eager, bald man, wearing a blue tail-coat, black pantaloons and an expansive white waistcoat, bustled into the coach. He was a little older than Mollie, and seemed to be full of self-importance. Several times he stared hard at Laetitia and however much she tried to hide her features by looking away, he was forever speaking to her or to Mollie, claiming attention in one of the casual ways which fellow travellers are at liberty to do and scrutinizing her closely. First he asked her, 'Did she not reside near Malton?' and then, further, 'Did she not have the acquaintance of the Misses Godwin?' so that Laetitia was frightened into believing he knew who she was.

Mollie attempted to distract him by enquiring, in her turn, whether he was on a tour of the country and whom did she have the pleasure of addressing? He replied to this that he was Godfrey Skellow, that his residence was near Doncaster – saying this in a tone of surprise that she did not know it already – and that he was, as she rightly guessed, on a tour of the country.

'I have just been visiting Rudston, to see the great standing stone there. You will no doubt realize, ma'am, that the first objects of idolatry throughout the world seem to have been plain unwrought stones placed in the ground as emblems of the generative or procreative powers of nature. They came at last to denote eternal life.'

'Oh?' said Mollie faintly, hoping that Laetitia did not fully understand what he meant. Their fellow passengers looked puzzled.

'In my opinion one of the most curious is in the churchyard of the village of Rudston. It is twenty-four feet high above ground and is of a very hard kind of stone. The weight of it has been computed at upward of forty tons,' Mr Skellow added, looking in his pocket notebook.

'You made the journey solely on account of this stone, Mr Skellow?' asked Mollie in surprise.

'Yes. I am writing a book in which it is to be mentioned. Probably I will hire an artist to visit it and furnish me with a pictorial representation.'

'That explains your interest,' said Mollie, smiling. 'I do not recall ever having met an author before, though my delight is in reading.'

'When my book is finished and published I hope that you will do me the favour of reading it.'

'What is the title to be?'

'*The Celtic Druids.*' Sensing an audience, Mr Skellow tucked his thumbs into his waistcoat pockets and was ready to expound his theories. 'It is my argument in the work, to show that the Druids of the British Isles were the priests of a very ancient nation called Celtae. That these Celtae were a colony from the first race of people, descendants of the persons who escaped the flood or deluge on the borders of the Caspian sea.'

'You mean that they travelled from that part of the world?' asked Mollie in a puzzled tone.

'Part of them travelled along the forty-fifth parallel of north latitude, becoming the earliest occupiers of Greece, Italy, France and Britain.'

The rest of the coach had already stopped listening, but Mollie, having been shut away from society in Cherry Wigston for so long, was enjoying hearing his talk and asked, 'Were there any other such peoples?'

'Others travelled in a southern line through Asia, peopling Syria as they went and arriving in Africa, then going through the Pillars of Hercules to Britain.' Responding to Mollie's fascinated eyes, Mr Skellow was encouraged to go on to give her a very tolerable resumé of his ideas on the standing stone of Rudston, which was at that time his particular interest. Then some chance association of ideas led him to mention Ramillies.

Even Mollie's attention had been flagging, but it was immediately restored, as he said, 'If only the Earls of the Ainsty had seen fit to build a replica of Stonehenge or Avebury! I could have given them the benefit of my advice as to the best site for such an erection. A great deal of money has been spent by various Earls on ornaments of the park at Ramillies, and a stone circle would have been of all things the most appropriate.'

'What benefit would it have been?'

Mr Skellow's thumbs went even deeper into his waistcoat pockets and he took a deep breath. 'Had we had a Stonehenge at Ramillies, we could have staged some of the old mystic rites of midsummer. I would have been willing to officiate myself, with a few accolytes,' he stared hard at Laetitia and she wondered if he thought her a suitable assistant in such play-acting. She shuddered and was glad that there was no such stone circle in Yorkshire. The man, for all his annoying personality, seemed to have a compelling power about him. She was not at all sure that if he demanded her presence at a midsummer rite, she would have the strength to resist. Fortunately the subject changed. Mr Skellow stopped staring at her with that hypnotic look and said to Mollie, who had told him her name and their destination, 'Scarborough is an excellent spa, Mrs Akeham. You are very wise to choose it. May I hope to meet you at the springs in the mornings? The north spring and the south spring have different qualities and your physician will advise you on which is best for your constitution. I favour the south spring and often come in the summer.'

Mollie wanted him to return to the subject of Ramillies. 'I understand you to say that there is no stone circle in the park at Ramillies, but tell me, sir, what ornaments does it possess?'

'There are many things, ma'am, and among them is a pyramid. Now if such a thing could be erected and money no object, why not a stone circle, I ask you? A pyramid is just such another symbol of ancient power. They have crowned St Anne's Hill with it. The very idea stirs my blood. I must ask permission to walk up to it. The new Earl is said to be amiable. I do not suppose he would refuse the request.'

'Going up to a pyramid seems an innocuous pursuit, sir.'

'Ha!' Mr Skellow looked out of his eye-corners at Mollie to see if she were being ironic at his expense. Her face was so serious that he gave her the benefit of the doubt. 'All my studies of the occult are harmless I would hope, madam. It would be possible to raise harmful powers. One must guard against that of course. But to raise benevolent spirits . . . those who guided the illustrious Greeks, or the gods of Egypt . . .'

'You are catholic in your tastes, sir. Egypt, ancient Britain, Greece – it is all one to you.' By now Mollie and Mr Skellow were having this conversation all to themselves. The other passengers were talking about the weather and only Laetitia was listening, in fascinated horror. There was something about Mr Skellow's personality which gave her an uneasy, repelled feeling.

'They were all most intimately connected,' he was saying. 'They knew powers that we know not of in our modern age. I have revealed a good deal by my studies. When my *Celtic Druids* is published I contemplate another book and think of calling it *An Attempt to Draw Aside the Saitic Veil of Isis*. What do you think of the title? It is not absolutely decided upon.'

'Now I understand your interest in the pyramid. Is that what you would do, given access to the pyramid at Ramillies, Mr Skellow? Try to draw aside the veil between us and the occult past?'

'There would be nothing hidden within it to give it the power of the Egyptian pyramids.' Mr Skellow sounded regretful. 'But the very representation of a thing has power in itself. Is that not so, madam – will not a portrait of a lovely young lady raise the passion of love in a young man who has never met her? Or, if she is his mistress, will not a portrait keep him faithful to her in absence? Yet this is nothing, only a representation. Just oil and pigment, wood, canvas or ivory. Can it be that there exists a representation without some of the power of the original? Would not a replica stone circle have acquired power? Will not the Ramillies pyramid have power because it is a representation of the power of the East and of ancient mysteries?'

'You have convinced me, sir,' sighed Mollie. 'I have a miniature of my late husband, now dead some twenty years and more. It does indeed have power, representation though it is of past reality. He stays young and I grow old, a widow for his sake. A quick glance is enough to remind me of the happiness I once had and can now only look to enjoy in heaven . . . That pyramid too may have some of the powers of what it models. We should beware, perhaps, of the representations with which we surround ourselves. They are not to be taken lightly. The Earls of the Ainsty should have thought carefully before inviting on to their premises a pyramid.'

'They invited much more than that, madam,' broke in Laetitia. 'They made their park itself a painting. The ornaments are incidents in a landscape. The golden dome of the pillared Mausoleum is placed where Claude would have wanted it and the Temple of Fortune crowns the spur on which it stands like a celestial culmination.' After this outburst, Laetitia fell silent, aware of Mr Skellow's renewed curiosity about her.

The last few miles flew by and the weariness at the end of a long journey was forgotten in the interest of running into Scarborough and pulling up outside the Plough. The landlord came rushing to meet the coach and to persuade them of the excellence of the dinner which was ready prepared to a turn in his inn.

Mr Skellow jumped out nimbly and helped down the lady passengers before waving his hat and setting off down the hill. Laetitia had shuddered briefly when his hand took hers to assist her down the steps and she was glad to see him go. Mollie in contrast had found him amusing and interesting and did not rebuff him when he hoped to see them again.

'Does not that man frighten you?' asked Laetitia in surprise.

'Why, no! Cannons frighten me, bayonets and bullets. I cannot find it in myself to fear phantoms raised in the imaginations of those who do not have enough to do.'

Laetitia shivered violently.

'Come inside, we will dine here,' said Mollie kindly, reaching out her hands to draw Laetitia's shawl more closely round her shoulders. 'You will see his talk in quite a different light when you have eaten. It was stuffy in the coach. The bracing sea air is now falling on your overheated frame. It is no wonder that you are giving way to fancies. We only had that slight refreshment at Malton. Come, my dear.' Her tone made Laetitia look up and accept this comfortable doctrine on the cause of her swirling fears and apprehensions. 'After dining we will have ample time to find lodgings in the town, rooms suitable for our stay. You will enjoy that.'

Laetitia remembered that it was she who was meant to be the companion to Mollie. Here she was being petted and looked after as though she were the daughter Mollie had longed for. How she wished she could be! How happy she would be then! The thought of Harry came into her mind and a quick blush rose to her cheek. If only she had never told him that she was the Countess of Elmet! If in truth she had been plain Miss Elmet, the librarian of Ramillies would have been a very suitable match and she could have lived so happily with Harry and Mollie in a little house on that beautiful estate.

At least she could make the best of her freedom for however long or short a time it might last and to do that she had a part to play. Laetitia determined to play the part of a companion to perfection.

She directed the inn-servants as to the disposition of their bags, ordered hot water to be taken to a retiring room for Mollie to refresh herself with before dining. She saw that, once seated at table, Mollie had all that she needed before the need was realized and she scolded the waiter in a way that would have amazed Lady Langbar if she could have heard it.

Mollie in her turn enjoyed the luxury of having her comfort considered at every turn and wished that Laetitia could be her daughter just as much as Laetitia wished it herself. What was Harry thinking about to only feel protective towards this delightful young creature! Why could he not have fallen in love with her instead of the village school mistress? If she had disliked the idea of Hannah Clare before, she did so much more now.

Harry on the contrary was more and more attracted to Hannah Clare as time went on. It was not difficult to see and talk to her often. Having been commanded to visit Ramillies with weekly reports on her pupils, she did so. In addition, Harry visited the school, inspected the work done there, heard the children read and examined them on their knowledge. It amused him and interested him. This was a world he knew well. He did not make much progress in his relationship with Hannah. On the surface she was always friendly and pleased to see him, but not only did he find himself subtly kept at arm's length but there was a sadness about her which troubled him.

One day Hannah complained about a broken window in the school house and Harry was for the first time admitted to that dwelling. He inspected the window, promised that the estate plumber and glazier should be dispatched to look at it, then made the most of his opportunity of being in Hannah's home at last.

'You are very cosy here, Miss Clare. It was in just such a cottage that I lived with my mother before I inherited Ramillies.'

'You, my lord!'

'I assure you. Just such a neat, compact little dwelling. Yours is, I think, rather the finer of the two.' Harry was looking particularly well that morning. His new clothes showed off the lithe and energetic lines of his figure. He had been doing more riding and his skin had acquired its attractive light tan. The corner of his mouth was crooking up slightly into the beginning of a smile. He went on,

'You have a row of books, I see, upon your shelf. May I claim the privilege of a friend and look at them?'

Hannah made an instinctive gesture as if to stop him, then dropped her hand, saying, 'It must be as your lordship pleases.'

He hesitated, but curiosity took him over to the shelf and he stood half turned away from her, looking at the titles.

'You read Tom Paine, I see.'

'My private reading does not affect my teaching in your school, Lord Ainsty.' Her voice was fragile with apprehension.

'Did I suggest that it did? You are too hasty in your own defence . . . I too have read Tom Paine though as it happens I do not own a copy . . . *Thoughts on the Education of Daughters* – Mary Wollstonecraft – very appropriate to your work here.'

'You will also notice my Bible and Prayer Book, my lord. You will see my copy of Bunyan, and Milton.'

'The cast of your mind appears to be very serious, Miss Clare,' said he, glancing at the changing emotions on her expressive face. 'The depth of your thought does you credit.' He turned back to her bookshelf. '*A Vindication of the Rights of Women* – another of Mrs Wollstonecraft's works. You are an admirer of hers, evidently.'

'I agree with her beliefs that a woman should be a free and independent being. We can see the drawbacks of our present system in the treatment being received by our poor Queen.'

'Is it your desire for independence which led you to become a schoolmistress?'

'It is a profession which offers what I seek.'

'Here in this school you are certainly independent yet your talents seem wasted. Should you not be running a private school of your own? You would not want for pupils. Or you could be a governess to the children of an influential family though that is not a position offering independence . . .'

'You are right in that supposition. I have some experience of being a governess.'

'Have you ever had the running of a private school?'

'No. My means would not allow the opening of one.'

'Yet you are a gentlewoman, Miss Clare. Have none of your family the money to help you?'

'Would that be independence, my lord?'

Harry felt baffled and looked at her wordless for a while. Then,

'It is usual to accept the help of wealthier members of the family if it puts one in the way of a lucrative business. One can pay them back, you know. They can regard it as an investment.'

'To accept financial help would be distasteful to me.'

Harry thought back to his mother's reaction to his newly-inherited wealth. He had understood it, because it arose from the natural, warm emotions of her heart, her loyalty to her dead husband. He felt respect for Hannah Clare's more intellectual objections to borrowing money. Standing with one well-shod foot in her hearth and an elbow resting on her chimney-piece, surveying now her bookshelves and now herself, Harry longed to know her better and to talk to her about the world and her ideas regarding the people in it and their relationships in society.

'Will you walk back to Ramillies with me, Miss Clare?' he asked. 'It is a beautiful day. I would enjoy your company and we could call on the estate plumber together. I happen to know that he is busy in the stables today. He could accompany you on your return.'

'This is generous,' Hannah could not help remarking when her long steps were keeping pace with his own. 'I would not have been surprised if you had asked me to resign my post after examining the contents of my bookshelf.'

'Do I strike you as so illiberal? No, I am pleased to find a rational, thinking being on my doorstep. I will look forward to many a friendly dispute with you. The word is friendly, you note. It was a great pleasure to me to find my cousin Peregrine in residence at Ramillies. He and I have views so different that we have many a great debate. Tell me, how did my cousin Joshua, the ninth Earl, react to your ideas?'

Her face was immediately rosy in a blush and her apparent contentment in his company vanished. Harry cursed himself for mentioning the man who always seemed to cause her embarrassment.

'The ninth Earl showed no interest in such matters,' she said stiffly.

'Did he ever enter your home, as I did today?' he asked, wishing all the time that he were not asking. He realized suddenly that he was jealous of his predecessor, who had known Hannah Clare before he himself had been aware of her existence. How had this intelligent girl reacted to that insensitive bully? The more Harry thought about

Hannah's reactions to any mention of the ninth Earl, the more he convinced himself that she must have found the man intolerable.

'He did enter the school-house, though not as you did.' Hannah was fighting to regain her self-control. 'He showed no interest of any kind in my bookshelf. For that matter, I never heard him mention having read a book. I certainly never saw him with one.'

'Why then did he come?' Harry wished the words unspoken. It was going to become obvious that he was thinking of her as a mate for himself and could not bear the thought that any other man had had the power he himself now held, the power of compelling her to see him.

'He came to see that the school was being run as it should be,' answered Hannah at last, now perfectly in control of herself, 'as you do.' The frosty note was back in her voice.

Harry decided to change the subject. He remembered that his mother was now at Scarborough, enjoying the spa waters.

'I was hoping that my cousin Peregrine and I might go on a day's expedition to the sea,' he said. 'My mother is staying at Scarborough and I would like you to meet her. When I was teaching she was always interested in my pupils and I know she will want to discuss our village school.'

Hannah hesitated. Then, 'I will be pleased to accompany you both.'

Harry was delighted. For the rest of the distance to the stables they talked on non-controversial matters such as education, and the plumber was found far too quickly for Harry.

When he returned to the house, he was reluctant to break the spell into which Hannah's company had locked him by seeking other human companionship. In particular, Peregrine's worldlywise, sardonic attitude was the last thing he wanted. So instead of going in search of his cousin he decided to walk up and down the antique gallery, getting to know his possessions a little better.

The gallery ran from one end to the other of the main block of the house behind the principal rooms. In the centre it met and became part of the great hall. From it rose the two unobtrusive staircases. This antique gallery was one of the unusual features of the house and within it, although so intimately connected with all the other parts, one felt isolated. Harry strolled up the length of it, then down again.

On either side were slabs of the most curious antique marble mounted as table tops. Some of them had inlays of semi-precious stones. On the walls above them were paintings, mosaics and bas-relief sculptures, and between them were statues on stands.

Harry drifted from one treasure to another. He paused in front of a basso-relievo of Victory, and reflected that he had gained a victory. Hannah Clare was to go with him to Scarborough, and to meet his mother. He inclined to venture. He almost decided to open his mind to her on that occasion and propose marriage. Oh, it was early. They had known one another no time at all. His mind had been made up, though, in the first interview. He almost thought it had been made up at first sight – when he had seen her with the line of children near the foot of the obelisk. He was sure no other woman would suit him so well. She would not be a mere bedfellow, but a companion for a thinking man, a mate in mind as well as body. She would give her children not only life but thought, principles and knowledge.

Harry went on drifting down the gallery, admiring the paintings by Raphael, Rubens, Bassan and others, and pausing to look at the busts of Cato, Junius Brutus, Homer and Hercules. The glowing colour of the marble-topped tables enlivened the gentle dimness of the gallery, and the soft reds and creams of the paintings contrasted with the greys of the sculpture and the walls. Everything there tended to refine, to uplift the mind and senses, and Harry was calmed by his reflective half-hour.

Then, as he was turning to leave, one sculpture caught his eye which was quite out of key with high-mindedness. It was in a shady alcove and was of a satyr, one of the mythical lustful, woodland beings, holding a goat. On the satyr's face was a smile which mocked Harry's mood, a wicked, slanting smile, and Harry was reminded of his strange cousin, of all those things which could set a sober world by its heels . . . He felt as though some emanation had hit him like a wanton, esoteric reminder that the world was not always ruled by its head . . .

Harry turned quickly and left the gallery. Reason and principle *should* prevail! The sober, the suitable, the wise! He would propose to Hannah Clare at Scarborough! What was that sound?

He moved to the window of the saloon – there was a sound, echoing across the park outside his windows – it sounded like Pan pipes, but that must be nonsense – it must be the wind – the wind tossing the trees by the south lake.

No Pan pipes, no wildness. Only the wind ruffling the surface of the water.

They set out for Scarborough in the barouche and began at dawn. The weather had decided to be perfect. They had the best horses in the north of England. The previous day a groom had gone on with a second team and stabled them half way along the route. Nothing was left to chance. There was a holiday atmosphere. Hannah smiled. They were to be some three hours on the journey.

Approaches to seaside towns from the landward side are seldom beautiful. Yet already the influence of the sea makes itself felt. Already it tempers the atmosphere. One begins to feel exhilarated and healthy. So felt the party of three from Ramillies as they drew up the long and tiring slope which would at last bring them in sight of their goal.

The view expanded; the sea spread before them. The rugged coast stretched away on their right hand and their left, and the great hill on which the remains of an ancient castle stood formed a background to the varied scene of huddled town and busy harbour.

CHAPTER EIGHT

SCARBOROUGH

Once the barouche was safely stabled at the Bull, Lord Ainsty, Mr Akeham and Miss Clare set out on foot to explore the town. They strolled along fashionable Newborough Street between tall houses built of dark-coloured brick with tiled roofs of the red of soldiers' coats. As they walked past the town's busiest shops they gradually descended a slope which would lead them to the sea. They all noticed the comfort of the excellent wide pavements and enjoyed the air of opulence and ease. It was only a few minutes walk before they arrived at the top of Bland's Cliff, a narrow dog-leg leading down to the sands and sea.

The tide was out and the great arc of sand shone white; very few people could have resisted it. They paused at the top of the descent and gazed over the ocean. So far there had been great harmony between the three of them, united in the pursuit of pleasure.

'Do we go down on to the sands?' asked Hannah without any hint of her usual reserve.

'You and my cousin may,' replied Harry, 'and I hope to later. But now I must go in search of my mother's lodging. During the day I hope that we will all meet – when she is prepared for company.'

'Does she not expect you?'

'She expects me, but I did not say which day, wanting to surprise her.'

Hannah looked, he thought, a little disapproving at this, but if there were a shade on her face, it passed quickly, and turning her head to the sea again, she remarked, 'I feel I could happily spend the rest of the day walking on those delightful sands.'

'We could certainly walk for a couple of hours, while you, my lord, enjoy the company of your mother and her young companion. The tide is out.'

Peregrine's tones held a suspicion of superciliousness, and for a second Harry hated him. He wished that he had not had to involve his cousin in Laetitia's little attempt to snatch freedom and happiness; the thought of Peregrine having the power to betray that innocent child, as Harry thought of her, twisted in his heart. His tone, however, was bright and pleasant as he said, 'Will you do that? I will ask my mother to join us for the meal we ordered at the Bull. Then there will be time for conversation before we set off for home.'

It was difficult to stand and watch the two of them walk down towards the sea, but a reward came, because Hannah turned, looked back at him, and, smiling, waved the light scarf she was wearing. 'My mother will love her at once,' thought Harry.

Then he turned to retrace his footsteps, going back along Newborough Street, away from the sea, until he reached the end of Long-Room-Street which was almost wholly given over to the accommodation of visitors.

He easily found the large and comfortable hotel where Mollie had taken a suite of rooms, and both she and Laetitia were at home, sitting in the window of their room on the first floor. The picturesque objects round Scarborough which were mentioned in the guide book were mostly visible from this window, and it had an excellent view of the sea.

'My boy!' cried Mollie. Her first thought was, 'He is just the same!' Just the same though they had been apart for over a month and so much had happened to him. Then her second thought came – 'He is totally changed!' – as after a greeting kiss she held him at arm's length and looked at him. Out loud she said, 'Oh, we are very fine!' and inwardly began to realize that his new position was bound to change him from the old Harry. With great responsibilities great good or great evil might result. His face looked more than a month older. He was more mature, more decisive; in that first minute his mother saw and thought many things.

'And you are fine, too, Mother! I see you have bought a new gown! You look very handsome in it.'

'Handsome, at my age! I have given up thought of being handsome, I should hope.'

'I teased her into it,' remarked Laetitia, coming forward from her seat. Harry had not neglected her. On his first arrival in the room he had looked over at her, nodded and smiled, before his mother had caught him in her arms. Now he had time to look at her properly, he saw with satisfaction that Laetitia's air was more confident than he remembered. As his mother released him, Harry turned to Laetitia with a warm smile and, holding out both his hands, clasped hers.

'How are you, Miss Elmet? You look as though Scarborough agreed with you . . . thank you for coaxing my mother into buying her new gown.'

'Scarborough does agree with me. My new life agrees with me. It is many years since I have felt as happy as during the last ten days.' She was amazingly pleased to see him again. He was, as his mother had said, very fine, compared to the Harry Akeham she had met in the church and at Langbar Hall. The old coat, which had been dear to her because it was the coat of her true friend, and because once she had been pressed to that rough tweed and found a refuge – the old coat had been replaced by one of the latest cut, immaculate and new. The old, well-worn shoes and hand-knit stockings had also been replaced by new ones of the finest quality. There was no doubt that he looked very handsome – and at this point Laetitia withdrew her hands gently from his clasp. She would grow used to his new appearance. Yes, he was – those clear, confident eyes, that smile – he was . . . he was handsome – yet she felt a twinge of regret.

Somehow they all sat down.

'I am surprised that you chose this large hotel,' Harry remarked to his mother. 'Is it not too much in the public eye to suit you?'

'Not at all. One can always live more privately in a large establishment. If we were the only boarders in a house our every action would have been remarked upon. But here we excite very little notice. We are only the two quiet ladies in number four. In wet weather we can promenade in the Assembly Rooms downstairs, and on the two days in the week that the Assemblies are held there we can go down, if we so desire, with no bother about chairs, or carriages, and return to our rooms when we have seen all we wish of local society, with no fuss at all. We can eat in our rooms, or if we choose, go down to the dining-room, which is spacious so we are not jostled close to other guests. The servants are all very obliging.'

'Have you made many acquaintances?'

'Scarborough is quite full – where is that news-sheet, Miss Elmet, with the list of notable visitors –'

'There is Sir Thomas and Lady Whichcote –'

'Oh, yes, and Colonel and Mrs Lloyd and their family –'

'The Honourable Mrs Langley and her suite –'

'And a good many others . . . we exchange the time of day . . . our closest acquaintance is Mr Skellow, Harry. You must meet him. He is full of the most curious notions! He is either a man of the deepest learning, or a learned blockhead. Miss Elmet thinks one thing, I the other: you must decide for us. You dislike him exceedingly, do you not, my dear, while I find him diverting. It is the only bone of contention between my companion and I.'

Mollie smiled happily at Harry and Laetitia, who were sitting quite unselfconsciously one at each end of the same sofa. She could not help being amused at the idea that the Earl and the Countess were pretending, for different reasons and to different people, to be a lady's companion and a librarian. She only hoped that she did not forget when and with whom they were which . . .

Two amiable women of good principles can find much pleasure in one another's society and she and Laetitia had grown very fond of one another. Their days had been full of many little domestic happenings as well as the bigger happenings of drinking the spa waters, promenading the streets and meeting the other visitors. The fond mother's stories of her only son had reached attentive ears and found an echo in the heart of the other.

The only shadow on Laetitia's happiness had been cast by their acquaintance of the coach, Godfrey Skellow. They were forever coming across him and he talked to them with great persistence – she wished he would not.

Mollie ordered tea and while they waited for it Harry asked, 'Can you still find the same sympathy for Queen Caroline, Mother, now that the scandalous nature of her conduct abroad has come to light? You will have seen what is being said of her in the papers.'

'It is the talk of Scarborough. Last week nothing else was spoken of. I am sorry, if it be true, that she should have lowered herself in such a way.'

'She is culpable, I fear.'

'I think we must consider her history. When she came over as a young, innocent girl to marry him she found him surrounded by mistresses and after the briefest of married lives she was slung off – there are no other words which can express it – by the Prince of Wales. While he was Regen the lived openly in a most depraved way and as far as I know her conduct was exemplary under great provocation.'

'While she was abroad her conduct does not appear to have been so. The reports are hardly fit for your ears, Miss Elmet. Mother, here is the tea.'

'It would not have been so bad,' remarked Mollie when Laetitia was out of the room fetching some dainty cakes they had purchased that morning in town, 'if the man in the case had not been a foreigner and a menial servant. I believe England would have forgiven her had he been an English aristocrat. As it is, though we must still feel for her as an ill-used woman, as a sister, there are many who condemn . . . there you are, my dear . . . you will like these, Harry.'

'The view from our window offers us endless amusement,' remarked Laetitia, noticing that Harry's eyes were drawn to it. 'To watch the varying moods of the sea would be enough in itself, for it is always providing something new; and in addition, ships are usually in sight.'

'Miss Elmet has counted as many as thirty all at once,' said Mollie before she began to bustle about her preparations to serve the tea. The teapot which had arrived under the escort of a servant had joined the cakes on a side table and Harry took the opportunity to speak in a low voice to Laetitia, saying, 'I know that you will not wish to meet my cousin, Miss Elmet.'

'No! Is he here? I had no idea of it.' She looked alarmed. No, she certainly did not wish to meet the Earl. The very thought brought back all the pressures which she had escaped.

'He is here. And so is Miss Clare, the schoolmistress from the village school at Anby. We made up a party for the excursion. You know Miss Clare, perhaps.'

'I don't think we have met.'

'She is a gentlewoman, and I think you would like one another. I hope to take my mother to meet them both, this afternoon. I suppose I cannot prevail upon you to make one of the party?'

'Mr Akeham! Are you forgetting? You know that I cannot, even if I wished to.' For a moment her eyes widened as she saw a threat to her new life.

'No, of course.' He had intended her to refuse, that was why he had asked her while Mollie was busy ministering to the teapot, and he imagined that he had managed the affair very nicely.

'I had planned to spend the afternoon on the beach gathering seaweeds, Scarborough is such an excellent place for them, and I am forming a collection. Please excuse me from the meeting; Mrs Akeham had promised me an afternoon of liberty today.' To Laetitia all time with Mollie had been liberty but as her employer was now free to listen and she wanted to be sure of not meeting the Earl, the girl produced a very convincing little bristle.

'You and I will have to go to the Bull on our own, Mother, as it seems you have given your companion permission to disport herself on the beach all afternoon.'

'Miss Elmet prefers not to meet much company,' answered his mother placidly.

'You will miss the excellent meal the Bull have promised to provide for us, Miss Elmet, and you will not be able to wave us off when we start our return journey,' he said in a mock-mournful tone.

Laetitia looked at him in astonishment, then saw his smile and discovered that he was teasing her. It was really not unpleasant! In the safety his presence brought her she could even enjoy raillery.

'I will miss it indeed. Your mother has been starving me, so much so that soon I will have to let out my gowns. And without my parting salute you will all be stuck fast, as if by an enchantment, and be unable to leave,' smiling in return, tossing her golden curls, and with a faint archness in the look she gave him from those untroubled blue eyes.

Harry wondered if among the gallants of the town she would find one who was both eligible and whom she could love. They would be hard to please if they were not attracted to so much sweetness and innocence. His mood continued to be one of teasing fondness. Was today not the day on which he was to propose marriage to Hannah Clare? As soon as his mother had met her and approved her, he would make some excuse to be alone with her and would then return to Ramillies the happiest of men.

When the interlude of tea was over he prepared to walk back to the Bull with his mother. As they walked along Newborough he took her hand and placed it within his arm. He was in high, tearing spirits, and would have it that he wanted to buy her something. He thought of all kinds of things which he might buy for her and she firmly refused all of them.

If she would not have a dozen bottles of brandy from Mr Allanson the spirit merchant, then he wanted to buy her a length of silk from Mr Estill the draper. If that would not suit, then he was all for commissioning a pair of slippers at Mr Percy's, some stays from Mr Tisseyman, or a flat-iron from Mr Lord. When she had resisted all these proffered delights, he came to a stop in front of the window of a jeweller's and nothing could move him.

'Will not the meal be ready at the Bull?' asked Mollie artfully.

'I'm sure it will' – with sadness – 'but I cannot leave Scarborough without buying you a gift, Mother; and you will not even accept a flat-iron, though I assure you I have enough money in my pocket to buy up a whole shopful of flat-irons.'

'Even if you have, it does not follow that I either want or need them.'

'Then dinner at the Bull must wait,' said he.

Mollie found that her son had indeed changed in their time apart. She looked up at this new Harry with his air of authority, and hesitated, and was lost.

'Come then,' she said. 'If it will make you happy, you may buy me something.' Harry joyfully whisked her inside Mr Cracknell's shop doorway and in no time she found a fine gold chain being placed around her neck.

'This is not a flat-iron,' protested Mollie feebly.

'To be sure it is. The very flattest of flat-irons,' retorted her son, giving her a kiss. 'You must have something to mark this day. It is a momentous one.'

When they arrived at the Bull, he asked for Lord Ainsty's private parlour and mother and son were ushered into a room where the table was already set and where both Hannah and Peregrine were waiting for them.

Harry could never understand, afterwards, why his mother took such an instant dislike to Hannah Clare. The sea air and breezes had brought a becoming flush to Hannah's usually pale cheeks – her whole aspect was bright and glowing – she had a bloom new to her. Yet Mollie's hand gripped Harry's arm a little tighter as he presented Miss Clare to her, and there was a stiffness in her manner which was strange for Mollie.

Polite small-talk, brittle as glass, began to take place between the four. They all exerted themselves. Each remark was a clear shining glass straw laid one upon the other to make a cat's cradle which would be shattered by any lack of caution.

'The views here are most extensive,' remarked Hannah.

'We find them charming,' added Peregrine.

He and Hannah appeared to be well satisfied with one another's company, thought Harry angrily, then at once took himself to task. Was he jealous? Of course not. He had always realized that the two were old friends. None the less, Harry wished that afternoon that his *roué* of a cousin was anywhere but at Scarborough.

'Such gleaming white sands! It is a pleasure to walk on them.'

'There are beautiful seaweeds to be collected on the rocks,' commented Mollie.

'It is delightful to meet you at last, Mrs Akeham. Lord Ainsty has often spoken of you. When are you coming to Ramillies?'

'Perhaps quite soon,' said Mollie, who was gradually accepting Harry's inheritance and now felt that things might be going on which she would rather know about. 'An acquaintance of mine here, a Mr Godfrey Skellow, has intrigued me. He talks much of the ornaments of the park. I told him you were to be here, Harry, today.'

'I met him some years ago,' said Peregrine thoughtfully. 'The ancient mysteries fascinate him as they do some others of us.' His eyes narrowed and glinted.

'He is sorry that you have no replica of Stonehenge, Harry, or he might have been allowed to stage Druidical rites.'

'He must be unsettled in his wits.'

'No, Harry, I assure you.'

'Mr Skellow has the reputation of deep learning.'

It was a relief when the inn servants appeared with the final dishes for the repast. This brought occupation. While they were busy dealing with the roast and the steaming vegetables, conversation was limited.

What remarks there were turned on the events of the day – the Coronation, now proposed for the first of August – the suggestion of the King's that the Queen be deprived of her title of Queen and the marriage annulled – the Queen's cross-petition . . .

'Is this not a demonstration,' said Hannah, 'of the evils of marriage in our society?'

'Do you not believe in the institution of marriage, Miss Clare?'

'I believe that women should be independent,' and Hannah's neck stiffened to hold her head at a proud angle.

'How can they be?' Mollie asked, astonished. 'What more dependent thing is there than a woman when she is bearing and bringing up her children?'

'Oh, but she should be independent! Marriage should not be what it is now, just a matter of property. It should exist only when mutual love and regard exist, and not be rooted in property. There has been no such regard for years between the King and the Queen. Marriage for them is a disastrous farce.'

'Surely – putting that case aside – the whole foundation of our society is the alliance expressed in marriage,' rejoined Mollie. 'The family is the unit, the property supports the family, and is passed on through it. Whatever one may think of such an arrangement, that is the fact.'

'It is not an arrangement which has my support.'

'Then would you support free love, Miss Clare?'

'If it would give women their independence.'

'It would not, you know,' Mollie shook her head. 'I never wanted to be independent of my husband. What we had we shared. However, had I not the support of marriage, I would have felt most insecure and unhappy. There were such women in plenty with the army, I assure you. With the officers as much as with the men. Women who gave all a wife gives without receiving the standing of wives. Very unhappy many of them were.'

'However have we come to be so serious?' cried Peregrine.

At that moment – they had finished eating and were sitting over fruits and wine – Godfrey Skellow was shown into the room.

'Dear madam,' he said to Mollie, 'I do not wish to intrude. But knowing that the Earl of the Ainsty was here, ventured to call. Could you introduce me?' His eyes had been travelling round the room and had come to rest on Harry. 'Your servant, sir . . .'

'May I present Mr Skellow,' said Mollie.

'I have heard of you, sir. Most pleased to make your acquaintance.'

'I have been travelling in Yorkshire, sir, studying the antiquities. Rudston was a place of attention and soon, after this holiday in Scarborough, where I come every year to drink the waters, I am travelling on to York. My journey will take me past Ramillies. May I have your permission to call and see its famous sights?'

'Visitors are welcome. I understand from my housekeeper that she frequently shows parties round the principal rooms and they are welcome to visit the park.'

'You are very good, sir.'

'Perhaps, Mr Skellow, you would care to accept the hospitality of Ramillies while you are in the neighbourhood?' went on Harry. 'It would be interesting to hear more of your opinions.'

'I would like that of all things,' said Skellow fervently.

Now that he had obtained an invitation to Ramillies, Harry expected Mr Skellow to go. It was with genuine desire to hear more of his ideas at some time in the future that he had issued the invitation. But today, as soon as the uninvited guest went, Harry planned somehow to take Hannah off alone and ask her to give up her prejudice against marriage and accept him. So how it was that they were all setting off together to Bean's Gardens, and there standing in a group listening to the antiquarian, he was afterwards unable to understand.

'What! Are there remains of Druids in York?' he heard Hannah asking.

'There are remains of the Culdees – hereditary priests – in both York and Ripon. The last Culdees of whom I have found any traces were in the church of St Peter at York in AD 936.'

'And the Druids?'

'These things are all connected. There is a Druidical temple at Brimham Craggs and as late as the year 786 the custom of lighting fires was continued there on the eve of the summer solstice. Of this, Hayman Rooke gave an account in his book *Archaeologia*.'

'This seems incredible. Am I right in thinking, Mr Skellow, that your belief is that the Druids and the Ancient Greeks came from the same original people?'

'The affinity between the Greek, the Roman and the Celtic languages observed by Mr Huddleston is consistent with my idea that a regular stream of emigration flowed from some great nation in the East to the West – irrigating, if you will allow the expression, with small streamlets, the countries on either side of its course. Thus a branch went into Greece where it founded the Oracle of Delphi, said by Pausanias to have been founded by the Hyperborean Ollen.'

Harry thought grumpily that it was surprising that Mr Skellow had not broken his discourse into sections, each with a heading, and did not expect them to remember the whole thing and write an essay on it. But Hannah's fascination was obvious. She seemed to hang on every word.

'The Celtae, of course, were the first swarm from the parent hive.'

'They were streams a moment ago,' thought Harry.

'Virgil was a Celt and so was Guipho, the Praeceptor of Cicero and many other Romans. Divitiacus, Caesar's friend, was both a King and a Druid. I believe that the Umbri and Cimmerii of Italy were nothing but Cimbri or Cumbri, and Umbria got its name like the river (H)Umber, and North-HUMBER-land.'

'This is most interesting,' said Hannah earnestly, taking no notice of Harry's attempts to edge her away from the group and along an enticing grassy walk. 'I knew that the Romans were in York.'

'Remains of the worship of Mithras are found about York almost every day and in the centre of the city, in Aldborough, lie the remains of a heathen temple to Bacchus or Jupiter.'

As they pulled out of Scarborough on their way home that afternoon, Harry agreed that Yes, it had all been most interesting. There had been disappointments, but they were his private property. He tried not to spoil Hannah and Peregrine's enjoyment by looking serious. He could call on Hannah tomorrow. He could propose as well in Anby as in Scarborough. When she and his mother knew one another better they would love one another, he knew that.

At least there had been one positive pleasure in the day. He had seen Laetitia blooming in a way he had hardly dared hope for.

CHAPTER NINE

PROPOSALS

Hannah had risen at her customary hour, superintended the young girl who came in each morning from the neighbouring cottage to clean, then done an hour's music practice and read for her set time, before breakfasting. Then, the girl having long since departed, she washed her few dishes, put on a stout holland apron and some clogs and went out to spend the rest of the day in her garden.

Harry had been detained longer than he wished to be by his land agent, about the day-to-day affairs of the estate. At last he was free, and hastened to Anby.

'If you will allow me to say so, Miss Clare, that is a most becoming cap,' he remarked, entering her garden by the wicket gate.

'Good morning, Lord Ainsty. It is a most common and ordinary cap, as worn by countrywomen in the fields.'

'The effect of a cap, you know, depends mainly on the features under it,' replied Harry, then, with some alarm, 'Miss Clare, you are not so well as yesterday. Are you indisposed?'

'Am I pale?' She looked selfconscious. 'The journey and excitement of yesterday have tired me, I think. I was glad that the school is still on holiday and that the day could be spent quietly.'

'You are a peasant for the day, then. Where are you bound?' – as she seemed about to leave the garden – 'I will come with you and be a peasant too.' He took hold of her basket.

'I am going into your own woods. You will be able to prosecute me for a thief, I fear. There is a fine bed of primroses I know of and I intend to dig some of them for my garden.'

Harry felt like saying that she was welcome to the primroses, the wood in which they grew, his heart, his hand and the whole of Ramillies. There were a number of interested spectators round the village green, so he said none of these things. He held open the gate, smiled, and said that on this occasion at least she was safe from being transported for theft.

They went into the woods on the farthest side of the great north lake and walked for some time along pleasant narrow paths under the shade of the trees. The many sights and sounds of the woods, the bird calls and the small animals glimpsed here and there gave them plenty to talk of, and Harry wished that the walk could go on indefinitely. Hannah could not have wished the same, for she wasted no time; she led him by the most direct route to the clearing where lush green primrose leaves gave substance to Hannah's memory of their magnificence in the spring. She set to at once to dig and Harry found himself with nothing to do; whenever he tried to help he felt that he was getting in her way.

'I was hoping for a talk with you,' he said at last.

'Talk away,' replied Hannah, her eyes fixed on her task, presenting only the top of her bonnet to the view of her lover.

'It is with difficulty,' remarked Harry mildly, 'that one makes a declaration of love to the crown of a cap.'

That brought her up from her work; she gave him a sharp glance, and said, 'I was afraid of this.'

'Miss Clare, you cannot have failed to see how I admire you. Of all women, you are the one I would choose as my wife. I love you, I respect you; will you do me the honour of marrying me?' He tried to take her hand in his, but it remained resolutely on the handle of the spade.

'Lord Ainsty . . .' she hesitated. 'I have tried to avoid this. I had an inkling of the way your thoughts were turning. Does that sound immodest?'

'It sounds truthful and honest, and I love you for those qualities.'

'I did not wish you to think of me for your wife, and tried to prevent you declaring yourself, because I cannot accept you.'

He had never seriously thought of her refusing. He had been prepared for hesitation and coyness, but a plain, firm refusal was something he had not allowed himself to anticipate.

'May I ask why?'

'It is not yourself, Lord Ainsty. I hold you to be a pleasant and intelligent man and value the friendship you have extended to me. That friendship I accept as though we were both of the same sex. Yesterday I made it clear that I am against the very institution of marriage. I will struggle against any hardship or difficulty to keep my independence.'

He was silent for a while and looked down at the clods of disturbed earth, the uprooted primrose plants and the clean cutting edge of Hannah's spade.

'As far as independence goes,' he said at last, 'you could have a sum of money settled on you which would be yours to spend as you chose. You would have independence in the fullest measure. Your children – our children – would equally be beholden to no one. They could all have an independent income.'

'I am opposed to marriage because it is part of the whole system of the laws of property. They are the cause of the corruption of our society. I will have no part in it.'

'You do not wish to see your children wanting for nothing?'

'Lord Ainsty, I am opposed to the hereditary principle, to hereditary honours. They stand in the way of the advance of civilization.'

'You may be right,' said Harry a little helplessly. To be refused because she did not love him, that he could readily have understood; to be refused out of a dislike of the hereditary principle, that was much more difficult. He looked at Hannah's face and was convinced once more that she was a woman formed for tenderness and passion. He felt that she was a creature of great sensibility and feeling, and that she must be lonely in her self-chosen independence. Surely her motherly qualities would not be satisfied with the village children – would she not long for some of her own? He appealed once more to her maternal instincts.

'You should think of the welfare of your children.'

'I think of them; I think of protecting them from the evil effects of wealth on the characters of those born heir to it.'

Harry at once thought of his predecessor, his cousin. Something in the manner of her speaking those words on the effects of hereditary wealth brought him to mind. Were the effects evil? Then they must be guarded against.

'You have escaped those effects, my lord, because you were not brought up in the expectation or knowledge of an inheritance.'

'I was brought up in the expectation of always having to work for my bread and no doubt that was good for me . . . I have no habits of idleness, or of indulgence in luxury . . . but it is a narrowing life, Miss Clare! Never to have the means to buy books, to travel, to see fine buildings and paintings, or the beauties of other lands. Surely one can be happier living as I am now, at Ramillies. The refinements of life should not be scorned, I feel.'

'Oh, Lord Ainsty! How much we are at variance! How can you be happy when there are people in need?'

'I hope that I will be able to be of benefit to others.'

'What do you intend to do with Ramillies?'

'Enjoy and maintain it.'

'Now if, instead of your sweeping pleasure-grounds with their obelisks and temples put there only as objects for the eye, the ground were to be split up into small plots each with its own decent farmhouse! The stone of Ramillies would build many such! Then would you have a garden more inviting than Eden, a scene on which Plenty would smile.'

Harry, who had very much enjoyed the view from his windows that morning, imagined how it would look sprinkled with a dozen farmhouses, with corn growing by the river and cabbages in front of the windows of a depleted Ramillies; with farm carts rolling over the picturesque bridge and poultry scratching where velvet lawns now stretched. Involuntarily he shuddered.

'My tenants can surely be made happy without such a sacrifice.'

'Have you been happy since you inherited Ramillies?'

'Not altogether,' replied Harry truthfully. 'It has all seemed very strange and I have felt isolated. A mountain-top is a lonely place. My unhappiness, though – if that is not too strong a word – has not been due to inheriting in itself. Had I come here as the village schoolmaster – in your place – the causes for my unhappiness would have been just as real and the means of alleviating them less. Now that it is more familiar, I am soothed and cheered by the beauty in which I live. The sight of the park gives me endless delight. The elegancies of life at Ramillies please me.'

'Ah!' said Hannah, shaking her head as though he were truly a lost cause, and going on with her job of uprooting primrose plants. 'There, I think that is enough. You may pack them for me into the basket.'

Harry complied. He liked the touch of the plants, the soft, crumbly mould which had nourished them, and the vigour of their leaves, and he packed them into the basket carefully.

'You must allow me to carry them.'

'Well, I will, as you have only been a bystander in all the hard work.'

Together they walked slowly back along the way they had come, each immersed in their own thoughts. It was an uneasy journey. Harry felt sure that Hannah was a woman of passion as well as sense; she had at times a tender charm. Behind her self-discipline she must be warm and loving. He respected the strength of her opinions and even in the first wave of disappointment felt proud that she did him the justice of knowing that he would not change in his kindness towards her because she had refused him.

They arrived back at Hannah's gate and he bid her goodbye. Those villagers who were still about smiled in a knowing way at them both. Hannah's whole demeanour was so dignified that Harry was sure it would quell any speculation.

'It was a great pleasure to accompany you,' he said clearly and she dropped him a curtsey. It was only walking back towards Ramillies that Harry began to experience the depths of reaction. Ever since his first sight of her, he had wanted Hannah to be his wife, and now those hopes were at an end. She had spoken in too decided a tone for him to hope. The flash in her eye – the complete seriousness with which she had suggested that he split up Ramillies Park into smallholdings – her opinions on the evils of inheritance – her whole firmness and calmness, put hope out of the question. They were to be friends, it seemed, as though they were of the same sex, and that was to suffice him.

As he entered the lofty entrance hall of Ramillies and walked through into the dining-room, he felt profoundly alone. Footmen had swung open the door, maids and matrons were busy about the building, boys and men about the gardens and stables; somewhere – in the library no doubt – his cousin was occupied. Yet the Earl of the Ainsty was alone.

He tried to take comfort from the elegant apartment and walked down its twenty-eight foot length, admiring its pictures. Looking at the Zuccarelli landscapes, he imagined the shores of the lakes cut up into small fields. He looked at the ruins painted by Panini and wondered why none of his ancestors had reproduced them in the park. He could not help feeling moved by the majesty of Veronese's painting of Christ on the road to Emmaus and by the wealth of expression caught by Spagnolet in his painting of the Prodigal Son. For a few minutes he was motionless in front of this before wandering restlessly on. If only Hannah had consented, she could, in the future, have been here talking over the paintings with him.

Later he stopped in front of Tintoretto's 'Cupid and Psyche' and wished that he could add to the treasures of the house the tender, true and passionate love of two human beings for one another. The place cried out for the touch of a woman's hand on the piano, the patter of the feet of children, the lacy froth of a shawl thrown carelessly over the back of a chair and the happy greeting of any member of the family who had been absent.

'What do you think?' he asked of a fine bust of Marcus Aurelius which stood on one side of an urn of green granite. 'Mind, body and spirit,' he went on. 'She won't have me, you see.' Across at the other side of the urn was the flanking sculpture of a bacchante.

Harry wandered over to the fireplace, leaned on the marble chimney-piece, looked down at the fan of folded paper in the grate and was silent. It was a bitter hour for him and he brooded there, reluctant to seek human company, until it was time for dinner. 'I will dine in my room,' he announced, and throughout the evening and the solitary night he could feel no interest in anything around him.

Harry took horse next morning, refusing the company either of Peregrine or of a groom, and set out for Scarborough. He had spoken to no one of what had happened and now said only that he was going to see his mother. Peregrine reminded him that he had invited the two Misses Godwin to dine and would hardly be back to receive them, so Harry hastily asked him to make his apologies and deputize for him. 'Plead urgent business,' he asked, and without further words he departed.

By now Harry had done enough riding to be tolerably confident. He had abandoned the quiet hack and begun to ask for a magnificent gelding, which, while reasonably docile, was strong and spirited.

To Traveller the distance from Ramillies to Scarborough was nothing, and even to be asked to return in the same day, with a rider of Harry's weight, was easy work.

He found the two ladies were from home, believed to be walking on the beach, and, leaving a message at the hotel in case he missed them, he set off in pursuit on foot, having left Traveller at the Bull. The season was now at its height and walking towards the wells of the spa he was among a throng of gaily-dressed, happy people. Among them, coming towards him, he saw his mother and Laetitia and realized at once that something was wrong.

'Harry!' cried his mother. 'How lucky that you have come! I was planning to write to you as soon as I returned to our lodging. This morning I have had news of your uncle. He is very ill. Mary is having great difficulty in nursing him and thinks he may not last the week. We came out to take the air so that I could think of the best thing to do and I am now determined to set out for home at once. I have said farewell to those of our acquantance we have met with just now.'

'My poor uncle,' said Harry in concern. 'This is not unexpected, though. He is of a great age and has not been himself since his illness in the winter.'

'I did not expect him to go as suddenly as this,' replied Mollie.

'You will go at once?'

'Today's coach has already left. There is nothing I can do until tomorrow.'

Laetitia had gone on a little ahead, leaving the mother and son together.

'Nonsense! You will let me hire you the swiftest chaise to be had and many changes of horses. What is the point of fortune if one cannot make use of it to help in emergency?'

Mollie only considered for a moment. 'Very well, Harry. You are a good boy. Now, there is another consideration. What about our dear Laetitia? I am very fond of the child. Am I to take her with me?'

'I will find out what she wants to do.'

No more was said, for they were approaching the busy streets where private conversation was impossible. Laetitia had paused and was waiting for them.

'My dear,' said Mollie, 'it is all decided. I am to set off at once in as swift a chaise as can be found and Lord Ainsty is to pay for everything. I will be in Cherry Wigston by tomorrow. My only sorrow will be leaving you.'

'Cannot I come with you?' Laetitia's distress was obvious.

'Mother, you will have arrangements to make, packing to do. Can I borrow Miss Elmet from you for a while? We will walk up to the castle and talk about what is best for her.'

'Don't be too long though – yes – I will be glad to be alone for a short while –' By now they had reached the end of Long-Room-Street; Mollie went off towards the hotel and Harry and Laetitia turned to walk through the crowded town towards the high hill which was crowned by the ruined majesty of the castle. She hung on to his arm, almost in tears at first. They talked hardly at all. As they walked, Laetitia cheered a little. They could have struck up Dimple and Tollergate, but instead Harry chose to zigzag a way through the town, down Sepulcre Street to Church Street, then down the comparative width of Westgate to the canyon of Castlegate, and here the height of the castle towered over them and Harry looked for a way to enter. There seemed to be no way; they faced the abrupt rise of Castlegate and climbed their way upwards to the street named Paradise which led to the church and there saw a path up through trees, with the promise of leading into the fortress.

Laetitia had been very silent and so had Harry. Now they needed all their breath to climb and he held out his hands to help her. Together, without a word, they toiled upwards. At last they reached a high footpath which ran along the castle wall and saw the gateway ahead of them. They paused to rest, panting, and smiling at one another. They had enjoyed the climb. The bracing air seemed even cleaner and brighter here than it did on the beach. They were both at ease at that moment.

Once through the gateway and past the outer walls of the defences, they came out on to a high grassy plateau, above the town, above the sea, above everything except the ruined keep which now lay behind them. In passing they had marvelled at its antique strength, then turned their backs on it and strolled forward, revelling in the summer day with its boundless blue sky filled with fleecy clouds, the deeper shimmering blue of the sea, changing colour as they looked, and merging at its farthest rim into the sky itself.

It was risky to venture too near the edge of the plateau, so they only went near enough to watch the rolling breakers falling into foam and the alternately rising and falling soaring flight of the sea-birds. Far below them, and separated by the height of the sheer cliff, the water roared and swayed and the boats far out to sea trimmed their sails and tacked into the wind.

Harry breathed in and out in great gusts. This was what he had wanted, to be in a place where the wind blew free and troubles could be blown away.

'Are you warm enough?' He had noticed that Laetitia had gathered her shawl more tightly about her.

'Thank you, I am perfectly warm. If there were no breeze, it would be too hot up here. One is unprotected from the rays of the sun on this eminence. Any pretence of delicacy of complexion would be destroyed, if one stayed too long in the brilliance of this atmosphere.'

Harry, glancing sideways at her, thought that her complexion appeared to benefit from the light and exposure. It had the look of health and the glow of blood rising to the challenge of sea and air and sun. He could not help but think what a pleasant companion she was, how gentle. If it had been Laetitia he had proposed to, would she have refused him?

'What of my future, now that your mother is returning to Cherry Wigston?' asked Laetitia, and, in his hurt and soreness of heart, Harry replied, 'Entrust your future to me. Share my life . . . in short, marry me . . .'

He looked down at her disturbingly, broodingly. He had stopped walking, therefore so had she. He had turned towards her, so that they were standing close together. As she realized the import of his words she gave a sharp intake of breath that was almost a gasp, then dropped her eyes and gazed earnestly at the ground. She said nothing. At that moment Harry had forgotten completely that he was the Earl of the Ainsty and that she was the Countess of Elmet. He only saw the delicate creature who had once tumbled into his arms and claimed his protection, whose welfare had become his concern, whose increasing brightness and spirit gave him pleasure. His heart was very sore and he needed the love of a fellow creature . . .

Laetitia in her turn remembered very well that she was the Countess of Elmet and that this young man was only a minor connection of the Akeham family, employed in some capacity at Ramillies. He had said nothing of the social difference between them. He had asked her as an equal. To accept him was to renounce for ever her place in society and to face ostracism for his sake. Yet if she did not marry him, she would marry no one; her heart had told her that, during these weeks in Scarborough.

The silence between them had lasted an age, it seemed. Then she laid her hand timidly on his. 'I will accept your offer, upon one condition.'

'Yes?'

'That we keep it completely secret until after the marriage ceremony.'

He had not realized that he would feel so happy; the swell of joy floated him almost off the ground, as though he too were a seagull and could soar in this buoyant air. He drew Laetitia's hand within his arm and, close together, they walked on, over the short, close turf.

'You do not wish anyone to know?'

'Not until it is too late to stop it.'

He nearly told her then, the whole – who he was, and that no one would wish to stop it – then he realized that would mean a large public wedding and nothing would less suit his mood. Even now the magic silence between them was too precious to break with explanations.

'How then is it to be managed? My mother leaves Scarborough today.'

'I would like to be married in the church where first we met,' said Laetitia dreamily.

'And why not? That would be my choice too.'

'You must apply for a licence, Harry,' said Laetitia shyly, 'if it is to take place quickly, and otherwise I will not know what to do. I must return either to Langbar Hall – and I do not think I could bear it, after discovering the pleasures of being away – or I must go with your mother to the Midlands, or take up some work, in the interim.'

'A licence would enable us to marry very quickly.' Harry felt all the advantages of such a step. No elaborate arrangements.

Hannah would be amazed that so soon after proposing to her, he should appear on the scene married to another, but that would be better than the uncomfortableness of facing her as a rejected lover.

'Suppose you go with my mother on the first part of her journey, to York. She will hardly go further today, and that is the most convenient place for me to obtain a licence. It might be possible for us to be married tomorrow – I don't know how long these matters take – the next day at farthest. You would be safe, waiting at the George.'

Laetitia looked up at him, blushed, then looked away. He patted her hand where it lay on his arm. Life suddenly looked more cheerful.

They walked a little longer on the high plateau, in a strange area between earth and heaven, where nothing was quite like it is in more ordinary places, until Laetitia pointed out that if she were to leave Scarborough that day she would need to pack and set their rooms to rights, and Harry remembered that he had set off very early without breakfast, and found that he was feeling lightheaded, besides having a post-chaise to hire, with driver, and then himself ride back to Ramillies.

When Laetitia was on errands to do with all these preparations, Mollie took the opportunity to say to Harry, 'Laetitia tells me you have found a situation for her. By the radiance of her face – I am not stupid, you know, my son – I have drawn my own conclusions as to what it is. All is to be secret, is it?'

'Yes, Mother dear.'

'What has happened, then, to the other?'

'She has refused me.'

'Refused you!' One look at Harry's expression made Mollie feel she had better not comment further. She looked away and said, 'Ho hum,' then was silent.

'And yet I think it right to marry. My position is lonely, Mother. I would like a wife and children.'

'Laetitia has the truest and best of hearts. I think I know her feelings.'

'Dear child! How could anyone be unkind to her?'

No more was said. Before long Harry was seeing the two ladies on their way, and promising to be in York in time to set his mother on the second stage of her journey the following day. At last he mounted Traveller and turned his face towards Ramillies. He too had much to do in what remained of that day.

In the richly furnished saloon, Lord Langbar was waiting for him.

CHAPTER TEN

MARRIAGE

They had not met for some time. When Harry entered the room Lord Langbar, his hands clasped behind his back, was looking up towards the top of the tall walls. He turned, came over to Harry with outstretched hands, and said, 'That looks like a Rubens, Ainsty.'

'I believe it is,' replied Harry, with hardly a glance at the painting. If one has inherited the priceless Ramillies Rembrandts, Dürers and Leonardos, an acre or two of Rubens is neither here nor there. Harry was preoccupied with the events of the day. Mentally he was in Cherry Wigston with his sick uncle, on the York road with his mother and his affianced bride, anywhere but in the great saloon with Lord Langbar.

Lord Langbar himself seemed to be under some kind of strain, for after his first remark he hesitated, coughed and finally made a statement about the weather, to which Harry replied, 'It is very fine. I was at Scarborough today and we had excellent weather there – it was almost too hot. You will be anxious for news of your niece. She is in good health and spirits. My mother has found her presence a great comfort.'

'They like one another?'

'Very much.'

I will have to tell him I have proposed to Laetitia, thought Harry, feeling disinclined for the task.

'It is about my niece that I have come to talk to you,' went on Lord Langbar rather awkwardly. 'The fact is that we have had a visit from an old family friend. His talk has made Lady Langbar uneasy. You know how women worry about things.'

'Who is the friend? Do I know him?'

'Squire Skellow – from near Doncaster – we had not seen him for some years at Langbar, though I have seen him elsewhere from time to time. He seems to have met both your mother and my niece in Scarborough and to have become quite a friend of theirs – always to be in their company. It is his reports that have unsettled Lady Langbar.'

'I met him a few days ago. He is a philosopher, philanthropist, that sort of thing.'

'Oh, yes. Not long ago he was in York bothering away about the lunatic asylums. Now he is investigating ancient religions. Never rests, the fellow doesn't.'

'Lady Elmet spoke to me of him. She did not appear to take much pleasure in his company. She feared that he had recognized her.'

'I think he did, you know, though she was a child when they met before. The upshot of it is, Ainsty . . . we rather fear Letty might be compromised by the whole business of running away and staying incognito with your mother. It has a suspicious look.'

Harry looked across at the intelligent, aristocratic face of his visitor, and said, 'Suspicious in what way?'

'Not in any particular way. It just looks – well, to be vulgar – a bit fishy. Lady Langbar put it to me rather strongly that the best way out of it might be for you to offer for her. A private engagement would explain everything if it were to get about. Only a suggestion, you understand, of my wife's. You must not think we consider her at all compromised,' went on Lord Langbar in a way which made Harry sure that Lady Langbar at least did consider Laetitia just that. 'Not a bad match for you, if you had nothing else in mind.'

Lord Langbar had not liked the task of making such a visit and it had taken a long time for his lady to persuade him to it. As he sat and looked at Harry's face, while different expressions came and went over it, he wished he could read the other man's thoughts. At last Harry, whose gaze had been fixed on the coal-scuttle, recollected that Lord Langbar was waiting for an answer, looked back at him and smiled.

'If I am acceptable to you, sir –'

'We will be proud of the connection.' The older man leaned forward and held out his hand.

'If I were to obtain a licence, would you be agreeable to the marriage taking place very quietly?'

'Indeed.'

'Will you be my bondsman, Lord Langbar? You will need to come with me when I apply for the licence.'

'Delighted.'

'If t'were done, t'were better t'was done quickly.'

'I think so. Skellow happened to meet the Misses Godwin on his journeying and in spite of their loyalty to both our families, so good a suggestion of scandal will be too much for their discretion, I fear.'

Peregrine was the only one of the household to be told of the coming event. He leaned negligently against the back of a chair, took a pinch of snuff and raised his eyebrows.

'I thought . . .' he was silent. Then again, 'I thought . . .'

'You thought my mind was set on Miss Clare.'

'I must confess that I did. You have me quite confounded.'

'Miss Clare is not to be wooed from her independence, I believe.'

'Perhaps not by you, my lord.'

'Do you approve of my choice?'

'Oh, highly! Highly!'

Harry arrived at the George Inn, driving himself in the curricle, early the next morning. His mother kissed him fondly and pressed his hand.

'You know how pleased I am, my dear. She has said nothing to me, so I have pretended the most absolute ignorance, though her face alone would have told me the truth. I could not resist asking if the new post you had found for her was to her liking and she answered 'very much' – you are a lucky man, and I believe she is lucky too and that you will both be happy. If only I could stay to see you married! Poor Mary and Uncle Verity, they need me so at present. May I come to visit Ramillies as soon as I can be spared?'

'Mother! You know nothing would please me more. If you would make your home with us . . .'

'I will not promise that. I was born and would like to die in Cherry Wigston. I will visit, though; and will look forward to seeing my dear Laetitia almost as much as I will look forward to seeing you.

I must be truthful, you see. My pleasure in your company must always be the greater of the two, although I love her dearly.'

'Mother – I thank you. My best love to Uncle and to Mary. If they want anything in the way of help or comforts –'

'They have all they want.'

'Yet if there is any little thing – say it is from me –'

By now the chaise was ready to depart and Laetitia was coming out of the door of the George with the last of the parcels to be stowed in beside Mollie, who said a fond goodbye to both of them and drove off with her eyes filled with tears.

Laetitia, having been paid her salary by Mollie, had spent every last penny of it on a large pink bonnet tied under her chin with rose-coloured strings, a pair of dove-coloured shoes and some Limerick gloves. She was very quiet as Harry drove her to the ancient church which was to be the scene of her bridal. He looked at her several times to see that she was all right and her radiant blush answered him.

Concentrating on driving, he could only make a few everyday remarks from time to time. When it was over – when they were man and wife – the constraint would go, he felt sure.

The roads were dusty with the summer heat and it was refreshing to pass down the two steps into the cool dampness of the sacred building. Harry had arranged for the vicar to be waiting for them with his churchwarden and an old woman from a nearby cottage to act as witnesses. The ceremony passed without incident and was soon over. In no time they were both signing the register. It was irrevocable.

'It doesn't seem long since I married the ninth Earl here,' remarked the vicar chattily as he watched them. 'And now it is you, my lord. Very happy to be the instrument of your joy, Lord Ainsty, I am sure.'

Harry thought Laetitia even more silent as they left the church.

'Is anything the matter, my love?'

'He called you Lord Ainsty.'

'Yes.' Remembering that the matter had never been cleared up between them, Harry added, 'I am sorry that I have not explained it to you before. I know that you have been under a misapprehension. I inherited the Earldom. I am the tenth Earl. You must forgive me, love. It all arose because I was not used to being a person of any importance, or anything except plain Harry Akeham. When you asked me my name that was what I said. Then I realized that if you knew the truth you would not allow me to help you, and you needed someone.'

'Did my uncle, Lord Langbar, know of this?' Laetitia's voice was very small, very cold.

'Yes.'

'And my Aunt?' Even smaller, even colder.

'Not at first. She thought my cousin Peregrine Akeham to be the Earl, just as you did. I expect she knows now, though. Climb up, my dear. We must drive to Ramillies.'

'Which you own?'

'Yes.'

'Am I now the Countess of the Ainsty?'

'Lady Ainsty. Yes. I'm afraid you are, my dear.' Harry began to be apprehensive. Laetitia looked at the curricle as though she were in two minds about riding in it. Then she climbed up obediently. As Harry took the reins he glanced at her face and was appalled to see its stormy expression. There was no trace of the radiant look she had worn earlier.

'You are distressed. I admit I had forgotten you did not know, things have been so comfortable between us. It was wrong of me not to explain before. In these last few days the world has been upside down. Will you forgive me? Do you mind so much? We do not have to live at Ramillies if you will dislike it. Everything shall be as you wish.'

'Everything is not as I wish.' Laetitia was very remote. 'I have been deceived and hoodwinked by the very people in whom I trusted. Did your mother know of this? She must have known.'

'She was very distressed by my inheriting at all and refused to acknowledge it.'

'I have been deceived and made a fool of,' said Laetitia. Harry whipped up the horses and did not know what to reply. He reached out, sparing his left hand from the reins for a moment, to reassure her with a friendly handclasp, but this she did not allow. She removed her hand decisively from under his.

Lord Ainsty did not speak again or attempt to touch her hand, as he drove his bride to Ramillies. Laetitia's intense silence beside him drove home her distress. When he did venture a sideways look at her, her set white features within the clustering curls, surrounded by the flower trimmings of her bonnet, made him feel such remorse that he was sick in body with it.

How could he have been so insensitive? So wrapped up in his own rejection by Hannah that he could propose to and marry this girl out of hand as though her own feelings were of no importance? Had he ever stopped to consider what her feelings were? Answers – and more questions – came crowding in on him until he was in an abyss of self-blame.

Well, there they were, after all; what was to be done about the situation? And to this he could find no answer, as he steered the curricle down the lime avenue, past the stable block, and finally drew up, not with a flourish but with a subdued and merely practical cessation of motion, in front of the flights of steps up to the great main entrance to Ramillies. He turned to Laetitia.

'You have been allowed to believe that I was in the position my cousin occupies and that he was in mine. Was that so very terrible? Will you not forgive me?' Her eyes were stormy. 'You are too upset to talk now. Will you walk in to rest for a little? I am more sorry than I can say to have caused you this distress. It was lack of thought and not malice. When you have rested, we could walk in the garden and decide what course to take.'

What had he done? Laetitia told him.

'Lord Ainsty,' she said, 'you may have gained a Countess, but you have lost a wife.'

He climbed down from the vehicle; a groom appeared as though by magic at the horses' heads. Lord Ainsty went round to help Laetitia out. The weather was all smiles to welcome her. On this north side of the great building the shade of the massive stone walls was cool and refreshing.

Obediently she put her hand in his and climbed down, and together the two most miserable people in the world walked up the steps and in at the great door of their delightful palace.

'Fetch Mrs Gambol,' said Harry to the footman. Mrs Gambol appeared in an instant and saw the two of them standing in the magnificent hall as if they were the orphans of the storm. She had known Laetitia for many years.

'The Countess would like to rest, she is fatigued. Can you find her a suitable room, Mrs Gambol, and some refreshment?'

'Oh, my lady!' Mrs Gambol went up to her in a motherly way. Laetitia, white and trembling, looked in urgent need of care. 'The Rose Room; that is ready for use and pleasant, if you will follow me?' To the footman, 'Get Jane.' Jane came in a twinkling. 'Jane, fetch up the tea-kettle, the daintiest china; ask Cook what she has to go with it; something light, and suitable for my lady . . .' This in an aside, as she escorted Laetitia through the hall and up the stairs, with solicitous clucking noises.

Harry was conscious of a great feeling of relief. There was much to be said for being master of Ramillies. The machinery of luxury was always there to support one, to let no need or wish go unsatisfied.

After mounting the stairs to the first floor and reaching the sanctuary of the Rose Room, Laetitia was glad to sink into a silk-covered chair by the window and lean back. The Rose Room was a calming place. Soft creams and pinks supplied the colours; elegance was evident in the choice of furnishings, the placing of each piece in its relationship with every other. The gleams of sunlight on the shining glass covering the framed pastels on the walls were caught and echoed in the silvery looking-glass. She was almost certain that she had heard Mrs Gambol say, 'There, my love!' as she placed her in the chair, as though she had been a baby.

'Where shall I put the spirit stove, Mrs Gambol?' asked Jane the housemaid when she came in through the door with a loaded tray.

'Set it on the hearth, girl, quietly now. Let me take that china. That's right. That's lovely.'

Laetitia was conscious of the subdued bustle behind her, as she gazed out of the window. The park was drowsing in the summer's heat. Her hand, on the arm of the chair, lay in a bar of sunlight and she turned it over, catching the warmth of the sun in a cupped palm. Her head was as empty of thought as a new-born baby's. She was only aware of being in a state of misery, as though a black, wet little cloud were drawn right round her, in that sunny room.

'My lady,' said Mrs Gambol. Laetitia looked round. A small walnut table of exactly the right height was drawn up beside her, bearing a tiny melon-shaped teapot, a small fragile china cup and saucer and plate. The plate carried minute morsels of bread and butter and two small cakes, and there was a bowl with a few strawberries. Even in her misery, Laetitia could not help smiling at the thought that it was exactly like a dolls' tea party set for the most expensive and exquisite dolls. Mrs Gambol poured the tea; its fragrance reached her and she accepted the cup. Jane, her hands clasped over her apron, smiled in the background.

In spite of herself, Laetitia felt a little better for the tea. She could not resist trying a strawberry, and then another. It was really a very long time since early breakfast at the inn and without realizing it she was hungry.

'Please tell Cook this bread and butter is very good,' she said. Mrs Gambol stopped looking quite so anxious and beamed, in tune with Jane.

'We would be so proud if you were to try a cake,' she coaxed. ''Tis as light as a feather. It would mean a lot to Cook if your ladyship commended her cake. And it is such a pleasure to have your ladyship to look after again, and to see *you* with his lordship, instead of that – that Miss Clare.' It was only later that Laetitia recalled those words. Just now she was marvelling at herself. It was really very irrational, having been deceived and betrayed by all about her, to be sitting in a sunny window at Ramillies enjoying a sponge cake the size of a walnut and her third cup of tea. The body, she discovered, has a will of its own and always enjoys being made much of.

Outside the grass swept in smooth acres of green and as she sat idly on, both Mrs Gambol and Jane having quietly left her, she could see Harry – Lord Ainsty – strolling across it. He looked as miserable as he was no doubt feeling and every now and then he glanced up at the façade of Ramillies, as though he were wondering which was the window of the Rose Room and how she was faring within it. Once Laetitia drew back slightly, sure that he had seen her, but his gaze travelled on.

It was then that she realized that she would not, as she had decided in the first storm of emotion, run away and have the marriage annulled. For where was she to run? And if this marriage were no more – even if an annulment were possible, and she knew nothing about them – what would she do instead? The horror of being hawked round London as an eligible heiress would be on her again, worse, infinitely worse, because she would somehow have become less desirable in the eyes of the world.

This horrific prospect was not the real decider. The most crucial fact was that she admitted to herself that she loved Harry and did not want to leave him, false, abominable though he undoubtedly was, cruel, deceitful . . . looking so miserable out there on the immaculate grass . . .

It took a long time for Laetitia to bring herself to any kind of action. In the past she had suffered passively, or she had run away rather than take more suffering. Now she had fully to accept that running away would not help her. She had to look her problem in the face and eventually decide what she wanted and work towards attaining it. She sat in the sun for a further half hour before, seeing that Harry was still outside, she made herself get up and leave the house to join him. All the time, Mrs Gambol's chance mention of Hannah Clare was lurking in the back of her mind, ready to be remembered. Harry looked up at her with apprehension, but pleased that she had appeared, and that she had come to him.

'At the moment I feel as though I will never be able to forgive you. The very thing I have been trying to avoid, to escape which I fled from home.'

'Is that thing in itself so dreadful? Marrying the Earl of the Ainsty? You have been deceived, I grant you.'

'Bamboozled.'

'That is a word I would not have used. On my part it was quite without intending harm. I was your friend only. It is as recently as the last few days that I have ventured to think of marriage between us.'

'Oh!' she cried. 'This is monstrous!' Monstrous, that she should have felt so long ago that she could marry him and that he had only recently thought of her!

'I assure you!' he urged, thinking that he was not believed. 'Do you wish to return to Langbar Hall? I will not restrain you if that is your wish.'

She shuddered. 'Go back there! I would be a laughing stock!'

'Then will you remain here? Would you be willing to take your place as the Countess of the Ainsty? Are we not friends? Can we not live in amity?' The pleading in his clear eyes made her drop her own.

'We were friends.'

'And will be again, I hope.' Something in his voice touched her heart. 'Is this a dreadful place in which to live?'

'You know it is not. I once told you how beautiful I thought it . . .' She was confused. The church where she had tumbled into his arms, where they had earlier that very day been married, came too clearly into her mind. She remembered how she had tried to reconcile him to Ramillies, praising its beauty. How she had given herself away in that conversation! She blushed at the memory of it.

They were approaching the Mausoleum, where only a few weeks before the ninth Earl had been laid to rest.

'Which is so beautiful it makes the living envy the dead,' he quoted softly.

'If I could live with you only as a friend – if you had not tricked me into marriage –'

'If? What then?'

'It could have been a happy day, coming to Ramillies.'

'And now?'

'And now, I cannot forgive you.'

He looked at her and believed that her resolve was indeed firm. His action had hurt and insulted her. Nothing, he felt then, would alter her. The docile, amiable bride looked every bit as hard and positive as Hannah Clare had ever done.

'If you would be a friend, only a friend. Stay. Be the mistress of Ramillies and my friend.'

'It seems to be the only course open to me. To run away, for instance, would be pointless. Before, it offered hope. Day after day must be lived through.'

'We need not be alone together. At present my society may well be repugnant to you. I could go away and leave you here.'

'What kind of appearance would that have in the eyes of the world? To marry in secret and then part! Are you determined to heap insults upon me?' She gave way to tears.

'No! Of course not! Please don't . . . Tell me what you want. Should we invite people . . . make up a house-party . . .'

Laetitia, whose dream of heaven had been a humble cottage shared with Harry and Mollie, had to choose being the hostess of a gathering at Ramillies as the least objectionable of the evils offered to her. Being alone with Harry, which had been such a desirable state the day before, was now to be avoided at all costs.

'Very well then.'

'Would you like to invite Lord and Lady Langbar and their family?'

'No!' she said vehemently. How would she face any of her relatives ever again?

'My mother, as soon as she is free?'

After a pause she nodded slightly.

'You do realize,' he went on, 'that my cousin Peregrine lives at Ramillies – he that you took to be the earl –' She shot him a reproachful glance as she heard those words, and shuddered. 'He is not a bad sort of fellow, come! I had to persuade him to the play-acting, and he only consented for your sake.'

'Deceive me, for my sake!'

'It was not such a deception, for I had to grow into the role of Earl. It sat uneasy. The advice I received was conflicting. Your Uncle wanted to involve me in politics; Peregrine (who is, I grant you, a reformed rake – or perhaps I should say, a worn out man ruined by former dissipation) wanted me to plunge into debauchery; Miss Clare thought I should split up the estate among the cottagers and labourers. My mother did not want me to succeed at all. The household staff wanted me to be a worshipped figurehead. The stable staff thought races and horses should be the staple of my existence.'

'And what do you want?'

He looked at her quickly. She had not been able to avoid sounding interested.

'I don't know what I want.'

They were standing on the platform of the Mausoleum. He turned his back to one of the pillars encircling it and gazed over lake and parkland to Ramillies. From a distance the great house looked inert; only the flag fluttering languidly at the masthead gave an indication of life. 'Look at it!' He threw out his hands. 'Just standing there! Look at it!'

'It looks still,' she said reflectively, 'but it is pulsing with life. In the laundry maids will be going to and fro with baskets of linen, taking it to bleach on the grass or carrying it in to iron. The blacksmith is busy at his forge; I can pick out the thread of smoke from his hearth. The estate joiner will be in his workshop. The cook will be happy in the kitchens for I complimented her on her bread and on her cake. It is not a house, it is a town, with no need of the outside world.'

'Help me, Laetitia, though I do not deserve it,' he said.

They began to walk back towards Ramillies. A butterfly started up from their path and began its dancing, wayward flight.

'I have found that one can live through difficult circumstances more easily if one makes a pattern of one's time.' Laetitia proffered her own little crumb of advice uncertainly. Why should she help Harry? It was all too much.

'That is what you suggest?'

'It is.'

'Order my day, filling it with different activities in different parts of it? Live to my own timetable?'

'I think you would find it a help.'

'Are you going to stay and help me do it?'

'As a friend, Lord Ainsty.'

They paced slowly towards the house and Harry remembered the tone of voice which she had used after accepting his proposal of marriage. The low-spoken 'Harry', the shy pressure of her hand. Her present tone of voice was the only chill thing in a summer's day.

'May I announce our marriage?'

'It must be announced.'

CHAPTER ELEVEN

THE HOUSE-PARTY

Lord Ainsty began by announcing his marriage to the household staff, hastily assembled in the hall. He presented Laetitia as the new Cluntess of the Ainsty and her hand was cold and stiff in his.

There was a delighted murmur among the servants. Mrs Gambol and Jane were not the only ones who beamed in delight. Laetitia had many times visited Ramillies. Now she was amazed to discover that she was not only remembered – that she might have expected – but liked; nay, even loved. For a feeling of emotional warmth swept towards her like a wave.

'I know you will all help me to care for her,' said Harry at the end of his impromptu speech. Just then she looked in need of care; he was afraid that she might faint.

'Oh, the poor pretty,' whispered the cook to the scullery maid.

'Isn't she beautiful? And that bonnet,' said the under-housemaid to Jane, as they stood drinking a toast in wine conjured up in two seconds by Mr Bridges and served in a strange medley of glasses.

'Oh, yes,' Jane had a proprietorial air. 'It is a real love match.' A soft glow came into the eyes of the under-housemaid.

The following day the new-sprung hopes of the household were dashed by the manservant's report that, although Laetitia had undoubtedly slept in the great ornate bed in Harry's room, Lord Ainsty himself had occupied the small bed in the dressing-room next door. 'By the look of it he was there all night,' confided one footman to the other, and the faces of the female staff grew longer as the story spread. They had already been mentally stocking the nursery. It was even worse on the second and third mornings when the news was the same. There was something wrong, that was certain. No one witnessed even the slightest caress.

'They're not like us, you know,' confided Jane. 'Their life is a show. They are like actors. It wouldn't do for an Earl and Countess to be seen kissing and hugging and that.'

'They are such a lovely couple,' sighed the under-housemaid sentimentally. 'You know I did see him putting her shawl round her shoulders the other day, gentle, as though she might break.'

A feeling of gloom might have made itself felt in the household if there had not been immediate diversion. The prospect of a full nursery had no sooner glowed on the horizon that it had dimmed and vanished. But the news of a gathering house-party cheered them.

Laetitia and Harry breakfasted separately in their rooms, and at other meals Peregrine made a third – a third to whom Laetitia could not become accustomed. She told herself that there was no need to fear him. She was in no danger of being his wife, had never been in such danger in fact. The enforced intimacy of sharing daily life with him, though, was difficult for her – she could not like him. The arrogant supercilious air; the twisting scar; the glitter in his eyes when they rested on her – she became more silent in his presence. Other people to diffuse the group were soon looked on as an advantage, even by the shy Laetitia.

Harry had written instantly to his mother so that she had the news of the marriage before it appeared in the newspapers. He implored her to come for a long visit if her uncle was well enough to be left. She replied that her return to Cherry Wigston had been just in time; Uncle Verity had died soon after; in the last difficult days she had been able to be of help to Mary. Now they were in mourning and there was still a lot to do. When the new incumbent took over the parish Mary and she were thinking of making their home together. Yes, she would visit, as soon as she conveniently could.

Their first guest was Isabella Langbar, who paid a bride visit with her parents and was persuaded to stay.

Facing her Aunt for the first time after running away was so difficult for Laetitia that she unbent a little towards Harry.

'My lord,' said she, leaning hesitantly on the door jamb and and looking into the dressing-room, 'my Aunt has arrived. Pray accompany me to the saloon?'

Harry rose instantly from his writing-desk. 'Of course, my lady . . .' he slipped off his banyan and eased himself into a frock-coat. 'Will you take my arm?'

Laetitia was pleased that the two main staircases at Ramillies, one on either side of the hall, were secluded. She could not at the time have made a grand entrance down an imposing staircase. The memory of all the events which separated this meeting from her last sight of Lady Langbar made her tremble and she was glad to have the support of Harry's arm. Feeling her shaking, he put his other hand protectively over hers – they entered the saloon the very picture of a loving couple. Fears were making Laetitia's colour come and go and her alarm had brought tears to her eyes, making them brighter than ever. The casual observer might have thought her radiant.

Harry could tell as soon as they entered the room that all would be well. Again, their position in society would be an asset; married, Laetitia had more social consequence than single, and now that she was mistress of Ramillies, even Lady Langbar must treat her with respect.

'My dear niece,' said Lord Langbar, coming forward and embracing her. She returned the caress without loosing her hold on Harry's arm.

'My dear Lady Ainsty,' said Lady Langbar in a tone of deep satisfaction, giving her a formal peck.

'Letty,' cried Bella, coming forward when it was her turn, third, but at that time first in the welcome she received, for only then did Laetitia let go of Harry's arm and step forward, to be drowned in her cousin's embrace.

'My dear, what an enormous hat,' said Laetitia in a quite calm voice, when at length she disentangled herself.

'Hats are distinctly larger this year. You must follow the fashion, Letty. We will go shopping for one together. For you. You are a naughty puss! Why could you not have told us of your plans, then I could have been your bridesmaid?'

'You must blame me for that,' struck in Harry quickly. 'Knowing your cousin's reticence and how much it pains her to be in the public eye I tried to please her by having a private ceremony.'

'The Countess of the Ainsty and of Elmet cannot help but be in the public eye,' observed Lady Langbar.

'But how different, dear madam, now that it is all over. We may be private here in our own family party. None but those we wish to see will attend us. Lady Ainsty may choose her own time and place for mixing in company.'

Laetitia came near to forgiving Harry on the spot, for this.

Half an hour passed, not unpleasantly. Bella was given leave to visit. First she must return to Langbar Hall for her clothes and she was to bring all Laetitia's own possessions, clothes, books and so on, with her. When they waved away the Langbar carriage, the Earl and Countess were assured of the first guest for their house-party. The idea was that they should give a large dinner, and that as many as possible of the guests were to stay for the weekend, some of them for longer. Officially it was to celebrate their wedding.

Harry had begun to make the acquaintance of men of letters in the neighbourhood. There were a number of professional men and minor gentry with interests in philosophy, archaeology and the arts. His invitations to them to spend a weekend at Ramillies were eagerly accepted.

'We must ask the Misses Godwin,' said Laetitia.

Godfrey Skellow, passing Ramillies on his way from Scarborough to York and remembering Harry's invitation, appeared to make one more. When she caught a glimpse of him approaching, through the window, Laetitia's look of horror reminded Harry that of all people, the one she disliked with an almost superstitious fear was Squire Skellow – but it was too late to withdraw the invitation.

'There is someone else I would like to ask,' said Harry. His wife looked up from her needlework. Harry stood up and shifted uncomfortably about the room. 'The invitation had better come from you. At present the schoolchildren are needed to help with the harvest and school is closed while whole families are out in the fields. I would like you to invite Miss Clare, our schoolmistress.'

He had been thinking of Hannah Clare in the last day or two. Those clear grey eyes with their fringe of black had been haunting him. She would know by now of his marriage. There could be no possible harm in seeing her again! They could be even better friends now that she would have no fear of him proposing to her. Laetitia would enjoy Hannah's company as much as he did.

Lady Ainsty's eyes were back on the firescreen which she was embroidering in delicate silks.

'I will write to her today with an invitation,' was all that she said. But she remembered Mrs Gambol's mention of Hannah's name, and it occurred to her that if she herself insisted on remaining nothing but a friend to him, Harry might ultimately look elsewhere . . .

In a few hours they would be busy, with all their company arriving. The hustle and bustle would make them forget the difficulties of the situation between them.

All the best rooms in Ramillies were to be in use. Mollie had again written that she was not yet ready to leave Cherry Wigston. Her letter was addressed to Laetitia: 'Have you really got Mr Skellow to stay, when you dislike him? Harry would have quite understood, my dear, if you had said. How happy and comfortable we were at Scarborough! I wished then that you could be my daughter for ever; now that I have you, my heart is almost too full for words.' What could Laetitia do, but forgive her any part she had played in the deception? If Mollie had been present at that moment they would have hugged and kissed one another and perhaps wept too, just a little.

Since his first night at Ramillies, Harry had always insisted that the small private dining-room should be the one universally in use. That first experience of eating with Crump had given him a dislike of the state dining-room. It was a different matter, though, on the day of the celebratory dinner when every seat was in use and the damask was surrounded by friendly faces. He looked round at the assembled company with satisfaction.

Away down the length of the glittering silver and crystal, Laetitia was smiling. Her lovely shoulders were revealed above a low-cut gown; the depth of colour in her blue eyes was visible even at that distance; and her fair curls were dressed high and decorated with flowers. Bella, half way down the table, was wearing one of the new evening berets, a large affair of velvet. Headwear was growing, it seemed. Like mushrooms, thought Harry, smiling to himself as he looked for the Misses Godwin. They had trimmed up their old evening caps with immense bows of ribbon and large bunches of artificial flowers, and underneath these erections smiled complacently at their neighbours. Hannah, on the opposite side of the table to Bella, was wearing a low dress of flimsy-textured black. It was the first time Harry had seen her wearing such a thing, and he feasted his eyes on the beautiful modelling of her neck and shoulders, reluctantly feeling as bewitched as ever. It should be a happy evening. For most of those present it was to be so. Godfrey Skellow was in his element.

'The Mexicans,' Harry heard him say, 'had the knowledge of figures, the decimal calculation, but not of letters; their picture writing . . .' and there Harry lost the thread of Skellow's conversation until much later in the meal, when he caught another snatch of it. '. . . It is not many years since I got the first hint of a kind of building in Scotland called Vitrified Forts. Their walls consist of stones piled roughly upon one another and firmly cemented together by a matter that has been vitrified by fire . . .'

Laetitia's feelings were quite different to Harry's. Her determination to endure was strengthening her. Life had shown her that there were things worth striving and fighting for and that her ultimate reliance must be on herself. At her table there were three guests, Peregrine Akeham, Godfrey Skellow and Hannah Clare, whom she did not want in her life and actively wished would leave it. Looking at them in their various places among the other guests, they seemed to her to be enemies. Allies she had none. Harry she was keeping at arm's length; Mollie had not arrived; the Misses Godwin, dears though they were, could be of no real help to her. The rest of the company could not claim more than acquaintanceship. They would be bystanders and not participants in any conflict.

The meal was a long one and by the time the party left the table the summer sun was sinking and the heat was abating a little. It was a time when the coolness of the sculpture gallery was enticing and Harry found that a group of his guests had wandered in there and were standing listening to the excited voice of Godfrey Skellow, next to a statue of a seated goddess, Ceres, goddess of ploughing and of the corn. '. . . she was of course worshipped in Britain,' came the voice.

'My dear sir,' broke in Harry, looking at the statue of the goddess as she leaned gracefully forward, her right hand resting on a cornucopia, her left hand holding out a plate embossed in bas-relief with a formalized flower, her eyes fixed, intent it seemed on her worshippers of centuries before. 'My dear sir, how can you possibly think that the Druids knew of Ceres?'

'I will prove it to you, my lord. Our Druids were acquainted with the art of making gunpowder, or artificial thunder and lightning.

They kept the invention a secret. The priests of Delphos also knew it and kept it a secret. Storms of thunder and lightning drove away invaders who intended to plunder their temple. What can we imagine those to be, other than gunpowder? In the accounts we have of the mysteries of Ceres, the most wonderful part was this very same secret. The probationers were led for initiation into a part of the temple which was full of darkness and horror, then all of a sudden a strong light darted in on them, followed by a noise like thunder again and again! This was also a part of the mystery of the Egyptian Isis.'

'Perhaps the old priests of all these cults did know of gunpowder and keep it secret, but I don't see that –'

'Lucan describes the Druidical grove near Marseilles, saying that it is often shaken, and strangely moved, and dreadful sounds are heard from its caverns, and it is sometimes in a blaze without being consumed.'

'And because reports of all these rites indicate artificial thunder and lightning you identify them with each other?'

In the twilight the whole of the antique gallery seemed to be peopled by ghostly forms. Light hardly penetrated directly; the only windows were at the extreme ends of the great length; otherwise it was a matter of borrowed light, borrowed from flights of stairs, from the hall, from the windows of the rooms on the south side. Light that crept in furtively and did strange things to the denizens, making real men like ghosts and the sculptures live. Harry remembered how he had lingered here until he had been bewitched into hearing the sound of Pan pipes.

'Of course the Druids had telescopes,' Skellow was going on. 'The knowledge displayed by the ancients – the movements of the sun and moon in their cycles of nineteen and six hundred years . . .'

'What do you think of these theories?' Harry asked the man on his right, an architect from York, who shrugged his shoulders.

'Who can say? Once start delving into these ancient mysteries, who knows what may be true or not true?'

'There is something uncanny about it.'

'About what? Skellow's theories? I grant you that, my lord. It sends shivers up my spine to hear him. He is utterly convinced. You must make up your own mind. It will have more interest for you than for most of us.'

'How so?'

'Living in Ramillies.' They were now moving slowly along the corridor. 'You have so many relics here of Greece, Rome and Egypt in their classic days. It is living here with you.'

'Living with me in 1820!'

'Even so. Thirty years ago, when this house was built, it was much influenced by the classic arts and within it a fulcrum of time seems to have been created.'

They had paused before a small mosaic panel some two feet square. It was both mysterious and malignant. Giant heads lay about the ground among stone altars. Whole figures might have been making or accepting sacrifice.

Into the silence came a ripple of musical notes.

Harry shivered.

'Shall we go to listen?' said his companion. 'One of the ladies must be playing.'

All the gorgeous state rooms were open and in use and the doors from the saloon were open to the garden. People were strolling on the grass of the great lawn and in and out of the rooms in the velvet warmth of the summer evening.

Bella had suggested music, and in the music room Hannah was playing her harp by the light of the first candle to be lit that evening. Bending over the instrument, she moved her hands over the strings-producing ripples and cascades of sound. The candle-light gleamed on her white skin, her shoulders, bosom, neck, cheek, arms and hands, moving fluently as the music fell from her fingers.

There was a sharp intake of breath behind Harry's shoulder, a voice saying, 'A virgin plays to Apollo –' and Skellow pushed forward past him as though controlled by forces outside himself.

'If only she would have married me,' Harry could not prevent himself thinking, 'I could have seen her like this whenever I wished.'

Two people on the other side of the room were watching, not Hannah, but Lord Ainsty and his guest Godfrey Skellow. Laetitia had forgotten her hurt pride, at seeing the way Harry's eyes were looking at Hannah. Her own gaze, blue and piteous, was fixed on his face. Had she lost him?

Peregrine Akeham looked gloatingly at Godfrey Skellow, pleased, brooding and hawk-like. It was as though he could see what was coming.

Hannah came to the end of her piece, rose and refused with a firm shake of the head to play longer. Harry began to blame himself bitterly for still finding her fascinating. Bella moved the candle to the top of the square piano and sat down to play one of her pieces. When it was over, she asked Laetitia to play, organizing the company as firmly as her mother might have done.

Laetitia had never played for Harry, and he found himself hoping that she would accredit herself well. The candle gleamed on her golden curls. Harry was also trying to fight down the desire to hear Hannah play again, so that he could experience her strange witchery and hear her mysterious music once more. The whole company had not yet recovered from the effects of that harp music. There was an uncanny aura in the darkening room. Everyone was silent, waiting. Moths flew in through the window; the candle flame burned motionless, without a flicker.

Laetitia had seated herself and prepared her music and then paused. Harry felt that she was looking directly at him. He could not penetrate her mood; she seemed serious and austere, a soldier, about for the first time to go into battle.

Then Laetitia issued her challenge to Hannah, and it was the last thing anyone expected. Into the room broke a happy, tinkling, infectious dance tune, so normal, so bright, that the whole mood was transformed. It was an innocent dance as if it had come straight from Laetitia's heart. It was full of merriment. It was the sort of foot-tapping music which in less than half a minute had Bella setting to to roll up the carpet, and then, too impatient to be dancing to finish the task, taking hands with the nearest young man and beginning to dance in and out of the furniture. This is a celebration, said the music. Be happy.

The York architect took hold of the elder Miss Godwin, Godfrey Skellow took hold of Hannah, and in a twinkling the whole mood of the evening had changed and from then on there was no holding the party. After half an hour the younger Miss Godwin relieved Laetitia at the piano and Harry found himself dancing energetically around the great hall with his wife in his arms. Her blue satin dress swung out over her feet in their blue satin slippers and her cheeks soon became as rosy as the flowers in her hair.

It was if a madness had taken over the party. Couples danced down the steps into the garden, then danced on the shaven grass.

Couples danced down the antique gallery with no thought of Druids. They danced through the dining-room and library, through corridor and saloon, danced up one staircase and down the other, danced up to the side table where Mr Bridges was dispensing punch and danced off again sipping from tumblers of it as they went. They gyrated round chairs and tables, danced until they were dizzy. Then the carriages began to arrive for those revellers who lived near enough to travel home that night. They rolled off behind dancing horses through the half-dark of the summer's night. The housemaids danced in the kitchen, the footmen danced down the back-stairs, Mrs Gambol turned a few stately circles with the cook. Long after everyone else had collapsed exhausted, down in the stables a couple of the stable lads, some magic infecting them too, linked arms and galloped around in the moonlight, their steel-shod boots striking sparks from the cobbles.

Twenty-four hours later almost all the guests had departed. Even Bella, who had hoped to stay a week, had been called back home by the unexpected arrival there of her fiancé. The architect had gone back to his office, the lawyer to his deeds, the doctor to his rounds. A few guests stayed on, however.

Godfrey Skellow had not a claim on him in the world to compare with that of Ramillies. Harry had found it impossible to ask him to go. He was so interested and excited by everything: the pyramid, to which he insisted they all walked; the Mausoleum; the obelisk; the Temple of Fortune; and most of all the large quantity of antique objects brought to Ramillies by Harry's ancestors. It would have been cruelty to part him from these delights. Hannah Clare stayed on too. So did Miss Godwin and Miss Martha Godwin.

Miss Martha Godwin had been walking in the park in the morning, before the full heat of the day developed. The spacious beauty of the softly sculptured hills with their young springing trees was a refreshment to the spirit. She was returning by the main garden doors, leading into the saloon in the centre of the long south front of the house. A flight of wide, generous steps ran up to the doors from the grass, and at the foot of them Martha Godwin stood entranced.

A peacock in full glory stood on the topmost step displaying his tail which was spread to its full extent in a vast semi-circle behind him. It was a full minute before Miss Martha realized that he was not alone on the steps. Half hidden by his tail was one pea-hen and halfway down the flight was another. How insignificant they looked in comparison with the male! Drab brown creatures, modestly subdued. Martha turned her eyes again to that beautiful spread tail. The sun shone full upon it, bringing out the irridescence of the blue-green, the infinite number of other colours and shades which shimmered over the surface.

The peacock shook his tail so that all the quills rattled together with a sound like falling rain. He turned to one hen and showed her the glory of his plumage. She ignored him, gazing as if in a happy daydream across the park. He bent his tail forward until it was like an inverted bowl and shook his quills at her repeatedly until the sound was like the swish of sea waves on shingle, but she would not turn her head.

'How can you ignore him?' Martha asked the pea-hen reproachfully. The peacock, failing to win a glance, turned and paid court to the other hen, pacing sedately towards her. She instantly became very interested in the view over the edge of the steps down towards the basement windows. The peacock demonstrated his glory. Martha, who was all admiration, was of no importance in his eyes. He made his tail into a vibrating rainbow, but the hen took no notice. He retreated to the door, through which Martha had intended to enter the house, and spreading the great fan in the dazzling sunlight, stood motionless. Both hens studiously looked the other way. Then he made more approaches first to one and then to the other. One of the hens wandered down the steps to the grass and stood there gazing into space.

'I do believe,' said Miss Martha Godwin, when she reached the small dining-room, where a light repast of cold meat, salads, bread and bowls of strawberries was set out on the table, 'that your poor peacock is still displaying out there on the steps. I have been watching him this half hour and if I had not begun to feel the sun rather hot on my neck I would be there still. What a magnificent sight! There he stood at the door of Ramillies, for all the world as though he owned the place, and neither of those insignificant hens would even acknowledge his advances.'

'You should have come in earlier, sister,' said the elder Miss Godwin peevishly.

'That is the fate of we men,' said Harry, passing cream in a silver jug to Laetitia and strawberries to Hannah. 'We try to look important. Our womenfolk constantly cut us down to size. They regard our show-off ways with contempt. They are really the important ones. The peacock knows that with all his splendour he is no use without them.'

At that moment Godfrey Skellow, his smooth skull shining pink in excitement, burst into the room.

'My lord!' he cried. 'The most wonderful discovery! Do you know what you have in your house?'

CHAPTER TWELVE

DRUIDS AND DELPHI

'Do you know what you have in your house?' Godfrey Skellow asked again, wild with excitement.

'A good many things, Mr Skellow.'

'A good many wonderful things. Among them – I can hardly believe it – is –' and here he began to speak very slowly, drawing out each word, 'is the actual altar of the Oracle at Delphi.'

'Yes. I have seen it. It is impressive.'

'Impressive!' Mr Skellow was speechless. He could not command his thoughts enough to find adequate adjectives. At last he added, 'It is unbelievable.'

'Do I know it?' asked Laetitia.

Harry explained, 'It is a round pillar of stone, not very tall. Its associations and history make it significant.'

'The Greeks waited in front of it for the Oracle to read the future for them. The whole course of history could be changed.'

'Let us look at it,' said Hannah. The meal was over, and everyone present felt their curiosity stirred. Together they trooped along corridors and down steps until they reached the altar. In the broad light of an English summer day it looked neither awesome nor mysterious. It was smooth and well dressed at the front and rough at the back, with mouldings round the foot and three slight depressions in the top to hold a tripod of bronze where once had burned the sacred flame. They inspected the altar carefully and with interest, imagining in their various ways the cult of which it had been the centre.

Godfrey Skellow was still trembling with delighted anxiety. As soon as he realized just what he had found, a plan had formed for which he needed Harry's consent. He could not bear to think that permission might be refused.

'Hmmm,' said the elder Miss Godwin, trying to sound very learned, and the younger one spoke for them both when she said, 'I am pleased to have seen that, Mr Skellow. You are always discovering something of interest.' Then they both began to drift away down the corridor.

Skellow could wait no longer to speak to Harry. 'There has been a remarkable coming-together of events,' he began. 'There was I chancing to travel on the same coach as your dear mother and the dear Countess, and through them making your acquaintance, my lord. Then you were good enough to invite me to Ramillies.'

Harry murmured something about their pleasure in having such a learned guest.

'For years I have been attempting to discover the riddles of ancient religions and here I find evidence, and proof of my theories.'

'I don't see how,' answered Harry. Laetitia and Hannah were standing quietly listening.

'But my dear sir! Here your family have created an idyllic landscape and erected a pyramid, the symbol of Ancient Egypt, and two buildings inspired by the temples of Greece and Rome. Here within the house are many precious objects from Egypt, from Greece, from Rome. Altars to their deities, statues of the gods and stones wrested from their very fountains and shrines.'

'Yes,' agreed Harry, feeling uncomfortable.

'It is clear that you, I and these things so pregnant with the mysteries of another world have come together with a purpose.'

'What do you imagine that purpose to be?'

'I conceive that it is to re-enact those mysteries. To hear once again the Oracle of Delphi. To see the sacred fire!'

'You mean that you want all of us to act out the rites of worship to Apollo which once took place before this altar?'

'Yes, my lord,' said Skellow with a sigh of relief that the idea was at last out in the open.

As they had been talking, they had walked away from the altar stone and through the principal rooms of the house and down the steps into the garden. There was no sign of the peacock, who had grown tired of displaying to his indifferent hens.

The garden boasted few beds of flowers. Its beauty was of shorn grass, trees, water, vistas and prospects, although here and there a flowering plant flourished in a hidden border. The Misses Godwin had remained in the house, out of the glare of the early afternoon sun.

Laetitia thought that part of her personal battle was to be a good hostess, and she hid her hostile feelings towards Hannah as well as she could. Now she suggested that they both take their sewing to the shelter of a spreading tree, and Hannah agreed. There were seats out there in the shade and before long the two young women were established for the next hour or so.

Harry increasingly appreciated and valued Laetitia as he saw her tackling her new role. The constant battle and effort was hidden from him – he saw only the victories. In spite of this Hannah still fascinated him. Now as he and Skellow strolled over the grass, he was very much aware of the two at their needlework, sitting in the summer landscape, and of the fact that if they lifted their eyes from their work they would see him. He felt that if he were the peacock he would have rattled his beautiful feathers and that neither of them would have taken the slightest notice.

He returned to the discussion on Skellow's idea. For some reason he had not rejected it out of hand and sent the fellow packing.

'I don't see how you can,' he repeated. 'This is a Christian country. The pagan gods were defeated long ago. You cannot recreate what is dead.'

'How can you say that it is dead when it is all about you?'

'Perhaps the two streams exist side by side.'

'Of course they do. The original texts of our Bible are in Greek and Latin. Latin is the first thing we teach our sons at school, and the language of the church. The old culture lives, linking us with the Druids themselves. They taught the Romans to worship Ceres, they went to Delphi and tended the sacred fire. There are a thousand links. In bringing the altar and the other relics to Ramillies they were restored to their spiritual home.'

'What do you want to discover?'

'What puzzles me is why? What significance does it all have? For it must be significant. That is why I want to resurrect the Oracle of Delphi.'

'What would you do?' asked Harry doubtfully.

'Place the altar in the Temple of Fortune, offer sacrifices to Apollo, please him with music, and ask him to tell us the answer to the riddle.'

'How could you take the altar there? It is tremendously heavy.'

'Lord Ainsty! Your family move hillsides at their whim!'

'I suppose it would be possible with levers and a strong cart.' Peregrine Akeham appeared at their elbows from round the end of a yew hedge and joined them as Harry added, 'Re-enact the ancient rites of Apollo . . .'

'No,' he added firmly of a sudden. 'We would horrify the servants. They would think we were worshipping the devil.'

'No need for them to know,' said Peregrine carelessly, looking at his fingernails, and it never occurred to Harry to wonder how his cousin knew what they were talking about.

'How could they avoid knowing?'

'If you choose to move the altar, that is your prerogative. You can say that you propose to take supper in the Temple of Fortune and want to provide warmth and light by means of a fire in the bronze brazier on the altar. None of the servants understand what it is or what it was. It is a lump of stone to them with a grate on top,' advised Peregrine.

'Late at night?'

'A picnic, in our brief summer darkness. A desire to eat at midnight and then to wait for the dawn.'

Once started, the idea seemed to be impossible to stop.

'What are we, then?' cried Hannah, when all seven of them were assembled later in the afternoon and Mr Skellow was explaining the scheme. 'Hyperboreans?'

'Colonel Vallency has proved as clear as the sun at noon, that the ancient gods of the Greeks and Romans came from the Hyperboreans . . .' Skellow embarked on a long speech, explaining why he believed them to be dwellers in Britain and connected with the worship of Apollo. Harry came to with a start to realize that instead of listening to this learned discourse he had been watching Laetitia's profile and wondering what she thought to the idea of this play-acting.

'You might remember,' put in Peregrine languidly, 'the account of Diodorus Siculus. I looked it up this morning. Here it is.' He produced a volume and read, ' "Opposite to the coast of Gallica

Celtica there is an island in the ocean not smaller than Sicily, lying to the north, which is inhabited by the Hyperboreans, who are so named because they dwell beyond the north wind. This island is of a happy temperature, rich in soil and fruitful in everything . . . they venerate Apollo more than any other God. They are in a manner his priests . . . in this island there is a magnificent precinct of Apollo and a remarkable temple in a round form." '

'The Mausoleum,' breathed the elder Miss Godwin.

' "There is a city sacred to Apollo where most of the inhabitants are harpers who continually play their harps in the temple and sing hymns to the god." There are ample proofs here,' said Peregrine.

'Read us more,' said the younger Miss Godwin. Harry noticed uneasily that the only female present who did not seem in a trance over the whole idea was Laetitia. He almost thought she abhorred it. Had it not been for the coldness between them – had the original openness of communication not frozen into this dreadful rigidity – they would both have spoken their minds and the whole idea would have been nipped in the bud that day. The two Miss Godwins, dears that they were, would have taken part in almost anything in order to remain at Ramillies in a charming family party for a few more days. They had never in their lives had the opportunity to dress up and take part in a play, and this idea – so very classical, and quite chaste, my love – was the most exciting thing that had happened in their innocent lives.

' "It is also said",' went on Peregrine, ' "that the god Apollo visits the island once in a course of nineteen years . . . during the season of his appearance the god plays upon the harp and dances every night, from the vernal equinox till the rising of the pleides." '

Harry could not help wondering what pleasure his cousin was going to get from all this. Was it only a sardonic glee in seeing them all dress up and make fools of themselves? Or had he some other motive – an evil one – which could not be fathomed?

Godfrey Skellow broke in with another of his learned and boring speeches and Harry thought that he agreed with the conclusion Laetitia had come to, when after first meeting him she put him down as a learned blockhead. Well-meaning enough, but tampering with forces he did not understand.

'You will not forget,' broke in Peregrine, 'that we learn from Claudian, "*Pulcher Apollo Lustrat Hyperboreas Delphis Cessantibus aras*." When the god forsook Delphi he betook himself to the Hyperboreans.'

'Now the altar of the Oracle is returned to the home of the Oracle –'

'Why us?' exclaimed Harry. 'Why should we try to recreate his mysteries?'

'The Druids believed in the soul's transmigration after death from one body to another. Are we not the descendants of the ancient people, do we not live in their land? Are their souls not in us?'

'The people who live at the back of the North Wind,' said Hannah as though the idea appealed to her. Harry was surprised that she should be so fascinated by this mysticism.

'The extremes are beginning to bend to the circular form.' Peregrine Akeham said this very softly; Harry just caught the words and wondered what he meant.

They all became caught up, in the sublime summer weather, in their idea of the ancient world as it was to be re-enacted by them at Ramillies.

Sweating farm boys heaved and struggled with the altar, levering it with crowbars on to a sledge which was then pushed and pulled out into the open and on to a waiting cart with strong horses. They then drew it over the grass and up the hillside to where the Temple of Fortune stood on its eminence.

Not a word was heard from Hannah about the waste of labour all this represented. She did not protest about the frivolity of taking the boys from their work on the harvest. She seemed indeed much changed of late. Her opinions were heard less often and with less positive assertion. Harry, watching her, thought something was weighing on her spirits and affecting her health. At times she had all her old bloom, but at other times she looked white and ill. In throwing herself into the preparations she had the air of trying to forget troubles.

Of all the ornaments to the park at Ramillies, the Temple of Fortune was Harry's favourite. It was an exquisite little building, crowning an eminence at the east of the main house. He had walked up to it with Laetitia, starting from the level area of the South Lake and its pretty bridge. There was a broad grassy walk leading upwards on to the spur of higher land. This walk had a dark wood on one side, and on the other side was ornamented by urns and statues on pedestals. Each carved nymph or satyr marked a stage on the upward way.

They had found the walk had a feeling of significance about it. The wood on the left seemed to hint at sylvan mysteries and the statues to be symbols no one could interpret. As they had walked upward more and more of the parkland came into view and when they had emerged into the open area on the crest they would not have been surprised if a lightly-clad nymph had burst from the trees with a satyr in hot pursuit.

Now, following the farm cart up the incline, Harry remembered that walk with Laetitia. The horses arrived at the crown of the spur, sweating and straining in front of the cart. It was a place of wind and air. The farm boys, glancing up from their task, rested a minute and looked about them.

Only from here could it be seen that on the other side of the spur, the shaven grass became farmland, a patchwork of fields and meadows extending to the left. Now that it was harvest time groups of people were busy with the last of the hay, which had been much delayed by the rainy June. Men with sunburnt arms and open shirts, women with shady hats, and rosy laughing children, looked at this distance as picturesque as peasants in a pastoral.

Harry thought that his own farm boys, resting in front of the exquisite Temple of Fortune, looked as though they had come straight from a canvas.

'Barley's doing well this year,' said one.

'Look at Brow's big field! Look at that! If this weather holds they'll be finished by nightfall.' Then they saw Harry.

'We brung it up, my lord. Wheer does it want settin'?'

'Up here, please. In the Temple. Mr Skellow ought to be here making it ready for us.'

Skellow was. At that moment he opened the door of the Temple from the inside. He was saying to himself, 'The altar is brought to the Temple,' a clammy dampness covering his skin and his tongue briefly touching his lips. He fussed about as the boys, who had remembered to bring the sledge, heaved and grunted to get the inanimate thing up the steps to the temple door, inside and to the spot Skellow indicated. They slid it to the mosiac floor as though it were made of glass, then rocked it into position.

Harry had thought that an altar should be central in the temple but the altar from Delphi was obviously meant to have its rough unshaped back out of sight. Skellow had erected a screen in an appropriate place and the altar was set up in front of that. The screen's dim, darkish background increased the significance of the creamy stone below, the gleam of bronze above. When lit, the sacred fire would outline the tripod in shadow on the dull screen, on the walls, on the floor, on the ceiling . . .

'It is become a May game with us,' thought Harry. All the attention of the seven was taken up by it. They seemed to exist in a closed society within the larger society of Ramillies and quite shut off from the greater world outside.

Hannah spent her time finding pieces of music she considered suitable for the worship of Apollo and practising them on her harp. Laetitia, chancing to come into the Music Room, found Harry there with Hannah, turning over some sheets of music with her. Their heads were close together and they were utterly absorbed. The sound of the opening door reached them and they both turned.

Although their occupation had been blameless, Harry felt a sudden sense of guilt. Laetitia also seemed to feel something, as though she had created an unwelcome interruption. Harry came forward at once.

'Pray do not disturb yourself,' said Laetitia hastily. 'I would not have come in . . .'

'I was about to come in search of you, my love,' replied Harry. 'Can you spare me half an hour? You are settled now, Miss Clare, about that song, are you not?'

For a while Harry and his wife did not speak, Laetitia doing her best to appear calm and composed. Harry felt vaguely as though he had been caught out in some sin; yet he had not been much enjoying himself. He had been discovering increasingly that the time he spent in Laetitia's company, even though she was so withdrawn and reserved now with him, was pleasanter than the time he spent with Hannah.

The house-party had given him the opportunity to be much with Hannah and she had appeared to have quite forgotten his proposal to her and to treat him as a friend. Yet he felt that Laetitia had caught him out in wrong doing. Did his wife not deserve all his allegiance? Had she ever wronged him, as he had wronged and deceived her?

'You get on very agreeably with Miss Clare,' remarked Laetitia at last, those deep blue eyes looking at him calmly.

'She is intelligent and interesting.'

'Do you agree with her views?'

'Yours suit me better, as far as I know them,' and Harry discovered as he spoke the words that they were true. 'You will remember suggesting that I make a pattern of my day. Will it please you to know that the first half hour after waking I have been devoting to serious reading; I have then been going for half an hour's riding exercise before breakfast. Is that the kind of pattern you had in mind?'

Laetitia smiled. 'It sounds like an excellent practice.'

'And directly after breakfast I have been dealing with my letters for the day and seeing the agent. So that by the time you first see me, I have already accomplished something.'

She looked at him with the kind of shy friendliness he had first found in her. 'That is very good. Now . . . what was it you wished to see me about?'

'Nothing of great importance. I was only wondering what you were to wear for our play-acting.'

'Are we really expected to dress up as Greeks, or is it Romans?'

'It would please Mr Skellow.'

'Pleasing Godfrey Skellow has never been an object with me,' said Laetitia with a little edge of pride and fear creeping into her voice.

'He is a guest . . . we have now agreed to this reconstruction . . .' Harry felt far from sure himself of the wisdom of the proceedings.

After a speaking glance at him, and a pause, Laetitia said, 'It is providing a diversion, and is no doubt harmless.'

'So, what are you going to wear on this great occasion?'

'If you will appear draped in a sheet, Lord Ainsty, I will guarantee to do the same.'

'I would be most uncomfortable. Do you think that is necessary?'

She smiled and shook her curls at him, and he found that she looked more attractive in her cornette cap than Hannah had looked in her gardening headwear on the memorable occasion of the primrose expedition.

'I suppose you men will be excused, as usual. Our dear Miss

Godwin and Miss Martha are determined to dress like the goddess Ceres – nothing will stop them. Miss Clare and I are not prepared to be so extreme.'

'Well, if you are not to emulate the Graces and appear in sheets . . .'

'Flowers in the hair, I thought. A wreath or chaplet.'

'Very good.'

'A night shift would seem not unlike the right dress.'

Harry remarked slyly that he had no acquaintance with night shifts, and the colour came up into Laetitia's cheeks. But she answered in a very controlled way, 'They are much of a muchness. You must have seen many such garments drying on the hedgerows, or being washed and ironed.'

Harry, defeated, smiled and nodded.

'They are the ideal garment because one could wear a good deal underneath, you see. If we are not to start the rites until midnight we are all going to be cold, in spite of the heat of the weather.'

'You could top it with a simple wrap, a shawl or cloak. The ancients wore cloaks. Are you contributing to the music?'

'I don't wish to have my piano taken up to the Temple and I do not play the harp.'

'Miss Clare can see to that side of it. Are we all to sing?'

Godfrey Skellow, content to leave the music side to Miss Clare, was much concerned about the possibility of offering a sacrifice.

'Surely there is no need to shed blood,' said Harry.

'You think not?' Skellow was dubious. 'A bull would, I grant you, seem excessive. Something quite small – a goat?' wistfully. 'Failing all else – a cockerel?'

'Certainly not,' Harry was firm. 'Have you been discovering what was usual? I would have thought libations of wine, offerings of grain and fruits, would be all that is necessary. Whatever it may have been in the ancient world, England has been a Christian country for centuries. In acting out these rites for our amusement, we need not behave like savages.'

'I suppose,' Skellow sounded resigned, 'libations of flour, milk, eggs, herbs and simples have been traditional offerings. Raw cakes and lumps of dough.'

'Anything else you need?'

'We will have to find mistletoe, the plant both of the Druids and of Ulysses. Oak. No ceremony can take place without oak leaves, and peeled twigs of oak will be needed to feed the sacred fire. Bellows, for it must not be blown on by human breath. Vervain, selago, samulus, marchwort . . .'

'You should find many of those in the park. I don't know about mistletoe.'

'Akeham tells me he knows where I can find mistletoe.'

The day appointed arrived, dawned fine, and seemed to speed past in last minute preparations. The household only knew that the Earl and Countess, family and friends would be staying up all night to see the dawn and to enjoy midnight refreshments in the Temple of Fortune.

'Everyone to what he likes,' said Mrs Gambol with raised eyebrows.

'I likes my bed of a night,' replied Cook, who was puzzling over the request for small cakes made of flour and salt. 'Do they mean sponge cakes, or scones? There won't be much flavour in them, only made of flour and salt.'

'If the Countess catches cold,' went on Mrs Gambol aggressively, 'I won't be held responsible. Folks ought to have more sense.'

'Gentlefolks aren't noted for sense,' was the opinion of Cook.

Harry asked Godfrey Skellow who was to ask the question of Apollo.

'It is your place to ask, my lord. I will take the part of the priest, and interpret the answer of the priestess.'

'Who will be?'

'Miss Clare would please Apollo best, I am sure. I would have offered the honour to the Countess, but it must be a virgin, you see.' Harry said nothing. 'One class of Druidesses,' went on Skellow, 'did magical incantations, possessed an oracle, and vowed perpetual virginity.' Harry remembered some of Hannah's words and mentally agreed that she seemed ideal.

'We also believe that the Pythia was a virgin – at one stage she had to be over fifty –'

'Then you had better ask one of the Misses Godwin.'

Skellow had no wish to do this at all.

'It is very difficult. We will all be there, will all be taking part. As Miss Clare's harp will be the only musical instrument she appears to be the principal among the ladies.'

'And what question are you to ask?'

'Apollo is said to have hidden his golden arrow among the Hyperboreans.'

'What question?'

'First we must ask him to appear to us, then we could ask the whereabouts of the golden arrow.'

'Gold!' cried Harry in disgust. 'Is that all you can think of? Gold!'

'You don't understand, my lord. It is not the value of the golden arrow, ornament though it would be to Ramillies. It is the fact that to find it would prove all my theories without doubt.'

Everyone had a task, and Harry and Laetitia were to gather the oak sticks for the sacred fire and then free them of every scrap of bark. They wandered off together into the woods and soon collected a small pile.

'Let me do it,' said Laetitia.

'Your fingers are not strong enough. I have a penknife – let me,' and Harry felt like a boy again, sitting on the ground working with the twigs, while Laetitia sat on a fallen tree nearby and watched him. He was sure that there would never have been any problems between them if only they could always have been together in this simple way. If only they were both in the middling class of folk! Such people did not know how fortunate they were. Above poverty and below greatness. At that moment, as the sun filtered through the leaves and the birds sang, and as Laetitia watched him with a half-smile, Harry would have exchanged Ramillies willingly for a snug schoolmaster's house, a parson's establishment, or the minor competence of a country gentleman, with his orchard and his arbour and one horse in his stable, as long as the horse was Traveller, and as long as the wife in the picture was Laetitia . . .

They dined as usual at half-past six, lingering over the meal. Then the ladies went upstairs to change their clothing and the three men walked up to the Temple to check that all was in readiness. The pile of peeled oak stood ready. The altar, with a little kindling wood between the bars of its tripod, appeared to be waiting. The floor had been strewn with a scattering of leaves as though a light breeze had blown them there. Around the edge of the floor were a few cushions and low stools. It was perfect, in the way in which proportion and fitness for purpose bring about perfection – the way in which the long sweep of a cow's horn grows from its skull; the way an architrave fits round a door; the way a harvester throws up the last sheaf to complete a balanced waggon-load; the way in which a gleaming yolk and sparkling white fit into an egg.

Even while he thought this, Harry sensed danger and destruction, and wished heartily that he had not sanctioned the idea at all.

They went back to the house to wait for the sunset. Peregrine brought out some bottles of an old, rich, dark claret and poured it into seven glasses on a silver tray.

'Must we wait for darkness?'

'The secret mysteries of religion were always carried out by the light of lamps or torches.'

'It is the passive feminine principle,' put in Peregrine. 'Earth, water and darkness.'

The skies were gradually darkening. No one was inclined to speak further. They felt at once foolish and intent. A force was rising in them which bound them together, which was gradually superseding their individual wills.

'We are ready.' Miss Godwin had appeared unnoticed and behind her came her sister, Hannah, and Laetitia.

At any other time their appearance would have been startling. Now, as the rest of Ramillies went to bed, leaving only the great saloon still awake, the women seemed the embodiment of the evening.

The Misses Godwin were in flowing linen, bound under their bosoms by braid, and their hair – left uncovered – was decked with flowers.

'Miss Godwin, you are Ceres itself. Miss Clare, our virgin about to hymn Apollo – you look splendid. Miss Martha, my lady – you too look splendid.'

Peregrine passed round bumpers of wine.

Both Hannah and Laetitia wore simple gowns of white under softly draping cloaks of fine wool. Their hair was also uncovered and loose on their shoulders, one head shining guinea-gold and the other dusky, in the half-light almost black, both crowned by flowers.

By the time they had several times toasted the success of their enterprise, such night as there was to fall had fallen. Feeling faintly ridiculous, they set off across the grass towards the Temple of Fortune, carrying between them a plate of flat cakes, a basket of grapes, a slender bottle of wine and a small pitcher of milk. The rising moon became strong enough to silver the sward and cast velvet shadows from every statue and tree. As they approached the long rising walk Harry realized that at night it was a very different place. If in the sunlight he had imagined satyrs chasing nymphs from the forest, his imaginings now took on more manic tones; not nymphs, but maenads. Had screams risen from the black depths of the flanking wood it would not have been unexpected. Only the outer trunks were bone white by the light of the moon.

Harry reached for Laetitia's hand and found her fingers cold and trembling. As they passed the statues and urns, they seemed to beckon or warn in the shifting light. Laetitia let Harry retain his hold on her hand and her fingers clung to his.

Godfrey Skellow was the only one of the party to be unaffected. He trotted ahead of them, a self-satisfied man, looking forward eagerly to reaching the Temple.

CHAPTER THIRTEEN

APOLLO

They left the glowering neighbourhood of the wood and emerged on to the hilltop where silvery washes of light were all about them. The countryside stretched away, mysteriously veiled in shadow. The Temple seemed larger, more dominating, than by day and infinitely more beautiful. As much more beautiful as marble is to granite. A beauty seeming to belong not to this world but to an ideal order of creation.

Godfrey Skellow moved ahead, propped the Temple door open to the night and vanished within. The others stumbled up the steps and could not see him in the darkness. They waited at the entrance in a fearful group, suddenly hesitant to go further.

Then there was a flicker of light in the dark interior and they saw that Skellow had somehow robed himself. The mundane frock coat was gone and his pudgy arms rose from loose folds of drapery as he lit the sacred fire on the altar of the Oracle of Delphi. The flames caught; the fire was fed with the peeled oak and blown by bellows, not by human breath, into a blaze.

They moved forward and as though it were foreordained took up their places . . .

Hannah Clare, the virgin priestess, sank on to a low stool directly in front of the altar and drew her fingers across the strings of her harp, making music which was one with the flickering flame. Laetitia followed her and stood at one side of the altar as a humble handmaiden of Apollo. Harry, standing back against the wall until it was time for him to put the question about the golden arrow, looked from one to another of them. He realized how divided he was. There was Hannah, who had caught his fancy so easily, the fire and ice maiden; and there was Laetitia, the gentle creature who had turned out to be strong and firm, the willow wand which bends before adversity but is not broken. He remembered that she had not withdrawn those cold and trembling fingers from his . . .

Peregrine was somewhere in the shadow, in his grey clothing melting into the background. Miss Godwin moved to the right of the altar, balancing Skellow on the left; she was carrying the wheat and wine, grapes and cakes which were the principal offerings. Miss Martha Godwin, forgotten by everyone, stood still in the doorway with her eyes rapt, inert.

Hannah began to sing to her own music and the other women joined softly in the melody. No one could have said how it was that instead of acting out a farce for their own amusement, the ritual seemed to have become real.

With glazed eyes Miss Martha Godwin took a step forward; two steps; she began to dance, her drapery of sheets turned to the folds of the chamlys. Through the open door Harry thought he heard other music, the thin clear haunting melody of the Pan pipes coming from another world, now lost, now heard again.

The men joined in the chant of the women to the melody of the harp as the night outside deepened. It was a long chanting as they stood or sat on the strewn herbs and oak leaves. Time seemed to be endless. It was perhaps an hour, perhaps two, perhaps time without end that they stood there with Martha Godwin twining and twisting between them and Hannah's melody spinning them into the heart of worship.

Laetitia had at first been thinking about her fear and distaste of the whole affair. Then, as she stood motionless, the music had caught her up in its rhythm. She felt tired, sleepy, hardly able to keep awake. Joining in the song they had all rehearsed together earlier, she found herself swaying in time to the music, drifting into a dream-like state. The flickering light mesmerized her into some kind of hypnosis.

Harry was trying to remember the question he was to ask. Every time he had it clear in his head it slipped out again and unbidden thoughts came in. The golden arrow, that was it. The arrow hidden by Apollo with the people who lived at the back of the North Wind. And another question – he had to ask the reason for the conjunction of time, the bringing together of all things, which had culminated in the seven of them being here at the dead of night in the Temple of Fortune.

A change approached, heralded by a sweet smell which spread through the Temple, seeming to come from the altar. It ravished the senses, giving exquisite pleasure, bringing images of celestial roses and lilies and many other flowers which only grow in the Elysian fields. The fragrance conjured up their presence as though the air within the space of the temple were crowded with incorporeal blossoms glowing with colour and light.

The time, everyone felt dimly, had come.

Godfrey Skellow stood forward ready to interpret the words of Apollo as they should be spoken through Hannah, the priestess.

Hannah left her harp and crossed to Miss Godwin, taking from her some of the offerings and went close to the altar. She prepared to cast cakes of flour and salt into the flames.

Before doing so, she stepped half a pace backward, looked up and cried out slowly, declaiming:

> 'By the bright circle of the golden sun,
> By the bright courses of the errant moon,
> By the dread potency of every star
> In the mysterious Zodiac's burning girth,
> By each and all of these supernal signs
> We do adjure thee, o great Apollo . . .'

The rest of the verse was never spoken. The Temple seemed to quake around them and, with a great flash of light and sound of thunder, to split open like a flower to the heavens.

The words which Harry was to use to ask the questions flew out of his head again. He looked up and saw the stars and the moon riding serene among her clouds, and then they were obscured by smoke drifting round in the centre of the Temple, what was left of it.

There was smoke, and as it cleared there was a great figure in front of him, that much was certain. A figure of a man, looming above all of them. Not merely as high as the Temple roof which had vanished in that great thunderous quake, but as high as the stars. Impalpable as a column of smoke, the figure yet glowed golden. Harry, awestruck and wondering, retained the memory of the perfectly proportioned feet, the lacing of the sandals – for these were what he saw when he looked downwards. That memory and the sensation of having been in a presence powerful beyond any imagining.

There was the feeling of great noise, hammering on the eardrums, making the head spin with waves of sound. The Temple itself seemed to shudder around them, one minute becoming dim as cloud, then firm and clear again in their sight.

When all this began Hannah had been standing straight and tall at the altar, about to make the libation and offering. She was hurled away, carried off her feet by the impact of the shock wave. It was as though she had been contemptuously thrown aside. Dashed across the room, she fell to the ground half in and half out of the Temple door. As she was thrown across the room the harp was in her path and was swept along with her to lie smashed and broken under her prostrate body. Her face was pressed to the scatter of leaves on the floor and her hands reached out over her head, the fingers scrabbling in supplication.

Martha Godwin had danced herself into a frenzy. Her hair fell wildly in all directions and her eyes were crazed. Now she fell to the ground near the altar, at the feet of that great figure, writhing, and with strange sounds coming from her lips.

Godfrey Skellow was standing unharmed with his hands covering his face, but at the first moan from Martha he dropped his hands.

The body of Apollo seemed to be obscured by smoke and become less distinct as Skellow began to interpret the words of the oracle, of which Martha was the chosen vessel. The voice was not his, but one of depth and sweetness, as her voice had not been hers, or the language English.

> 'And do you dare to mock Apollo's sacred shrine
> No virgin she you bring before the god divine . . .'

No virgin? Harry looked in consternation at Hannah Clare, lying sprawled on the floor not far from his feet. But –

'You and Godfrey Skellow were both taken in, were you not?' came a thin voice, like a snake's, thought Harry, if snakes had voices. Peregrine's voice rang, cold with malice, from the other side of Hannah's prone body.

The voice which was coming from Godfrey Skellow went on:

'With holy nuptial vows she took the bridal path
So seek you not to rouse the great Apollo's wrath . . .'

Again there came the sound as of thunder, the quaking of earth and sky, the fear and the amazement. It lasted long enough for them to feel that it might never end.

Laetitia alone was calm.

The flickering light was more like flashes of lightning that the light of the brazier fire. It lit up her golden hair decked with flowers, her white skin and white drapery. Her deep blue eyes, apparently unseeing, swept the temple and those in it. Stepping forward, she took Hannah's place.

'Thy servant, o great Apollo,' she said, and her voice was as clear as the moonlight, but dead and trancelike. It cut through the tumult like a sword, and sudden peace came after her words, and the scent of flowers was renewed and came like a garden after rain.

The vision of the towering god, cloudlike, golden, began to fade.

In complete silence Laetitia picked up the bellows and blew the fire in the tripod on the altar into renewed life and fed it with peeled oak twigs. Slowly, and giving each action the beauty of a symbolic sacrifice, she made the offerings. Into the flames she threw corn, grapes and the cakes of flour and salt. In front of the altar she made the libations by pouring first wine and then milk into a silver dish.

All this Laetitia did in complete silence. Taking courage, Harry stepped forward and asked his questions. Nothing seemed to happen. Then Martha Godwin shrieked and once more babbled unintelligibly. Godfrey Skellow translated and Harry thought he would never forget the singular sweetness of the voice.

'The arrow's lost, yet the next owner of this ground
Before the flight of the sea eagle will be found.'

Laetitia continued to feed the sacred fire. Godfrey Skellow in his own voice cried out praises and glorifications. Hannah scrabbled helplessly at the floor, sobbing.

Harry realized that the climax had passed. The god – if it had been the god – had withdrawn his presence from them – if he had been present –

He could not have said exactly when he first became aware that the gigantic figure was there no longer. He looked up and saw, not the starry skies, but the exquisitely moulded interior of the Temple of Fortune.

Laetitia stood still like an antique statue, her feet and lower limbs lit brilliantly by the moonlight striking through the window beside her. Her hand holding the silver pitcher could also be seen clearly. Harry knew rather than saw the grace of the rest of her figure. Then, seeming to wake, she looked round in surprise and hastily dropped the pitcher of milk.

Hannah sat up on the floor and wiped the tears from her face with a fold of her drapery.

The supernatural forces had ebbed from the Temple, leaving it high and dry, normal, almost cosy.

What was weird was the silence. Where all had been a riot of noise, movement and turbulence, now the moonlight penetrating the windows and the open door lay in an exquisite calm of silver sheets and outside the orb itself sailed in a cloudless sky. Looking from the windows, the seven could see the countryside around was as still as a painting. The trees held their leaves breathless against the heavens.

Godfrey Skellow was no longer a servant of Apollo but only a plumpish, middle-aged man with bare, flabby arms gleaming obscenely from the shadow.

'I would have offered the Countess the post of virgin priestess,' he said hastily to Harry, 'had I known that – but of course I thought –' A flush darkened the top of his skull.

Harry looked round at them all, a Harry they had not known before. He looked stern and autocratic. He gave Skellow a glance which made that gentleman shrink back against the wall.

'Revelations, eh, my lord?' said Peregrine, lounging forward into the central space. 'Is it over then? Very interesting, Mr Skellow. Amusing. The servants will have some tidying away to do.'

Harry ignored him.

Hannah Clare was still sitting on the floor amid the ruins of her harp.

'It seems to me that you have something to explain,' Harry said to her, and his voice was stern. He had loved this woman.

She would hardly have been recognized as the self-contained schoolmistress. She looked more like a piece of wreckage washed up by the tide.

'I hoped no one would know,' said Hannah like a sulky girl.

'You were my virgin,' Godfrey Skellow was reproachful. 'The Virgin of the Temple. Were we deceived in you?'

'I have been married,' she replied with some asperity. 'People who are married are not usually virgins,' and she looked meaningfully at Laetitia.

'Married!' Harry remembered her words to him in the primrose wood, and the words of the oracle, 'with holy nuptial vows she took the bridal path'. 'But you don't believe in marriage. Were you trying to avoid hurting me with the real reason for your refusal?'

'No,' Hannah's tone was vicious as though she wanted to cut him with the word. 'I am a widow. I was a widow then. I told you the truth. I do not believe in marriage. It means the end of all self-respect and the loss of independence.' She sat upright. 'I am deeply ashamed of myself for agreeing to it, for giving way. My heart and body betrayed me. Do you think I am proud of actions which my intellect does not approve?'

'Let us be clear. You have been married?'

'Yes! Yes! And I am carrying a child.'

At this point the two Misses Godwin, who had been looking round sheepishly, already finding it difficult to remember anything of the happenings of the night, began to take notice.

'How were you planning to manage?' asked Harry.

'Not by relying on anyone else, you may be sure,' said Hannah tartly. 'I have a friend who runs a boarding school for young ladies, who offered me asylum. I was intending to resign my post with you, Lord Ainsty, and leave at Christmas. My child will be born in the spring.'

'Spring?' Miss Godwin came and sat on the floor beside the girl. 'That is a great way off! Your widowhood must have been very recent?'

Outside the sky in the east was lightening to grey and inside the sacred fire was dying down. No one replenished it. As the minutes went by the clear dawn was strengthening and the moonlight paling. The contrasts between lightness and darkness were losing their force.

'It is recent.'

'We knew nothing of this,' said Miss Martha Godwin, quite her old self again. 'No one said you had been married. *Miss* Clare, you were understood to be.'

'I told him that I would not take his name or give up my place at the school.' Then, under her breath, 'Had he lived, things might have turned out differently.'

'This was a strange marriage,' said Skellow, wondering.

'Do you think I am proud of my weakness?' cried Hannah, and burst into sobs. 'Was it not enough to be betrayed by my passion for him, by my longing for his body? Do I have to proclaim my abasement from the housetops?'

Harry's voice was stern. 'Marriage is a matter for pride, do you not think that, Miss Clare? Is one not proud, to love and be loved? To claim one's mate in the eyes of the society in which as a couple, a household, perhaps at last a family, one will play one's part?'

'Is all success in achieving independence to be thrown away? My life work of teaching – I am a good teacher, Lord Ainsty, as you have recognized – to be abrogated? Was my position to be one of a servant to my bodily ardour – and to his –'

'You are a beautiful woman, Miss Clare,' said Godfrey Skellow who could not believe that beauty had any other end to serve. Had not all the ancient goddesses had a desire for fecundity?

'You must be broken-hearted at your husband's death,' said Miss Godwin tenderly. 'Was he ill long?'

'It was an accident,' curtly.

'We cannot go on calling you Miss Clare, as you are to become a mother. Please tell us by what name we are to call you,' asked Harry.

'I will not give up my name.'

'For heaven's sake!' Then, seeing a touch of humour in the situation, he went on, 'For the sake of Apollo! You must tell us, Miss Clare! This is absurd and ridiculous! I must insist that you tell us at once the name of your husband and the father of your child!'

Hannah turned her head away from him and after a few seconds she said, 'He was your cousin, Joshua Akeham.'

'The ninth Earl,' put in Peregrine.

'He was your cousin Joshua Akeham.' 'The ninth Earl.' These words ran round their heads like bowls down an alley or Jove's thunderbolts circling the sky, meaningless, lost in a vast exhaustion.

Their significance was too tremendous to absorb yet somehow it was already absorbed, had been no sooner said than believed, shedding light on attitudes and actions.

'This makes a great difference,' Harry heard himself saying. No one else spoke. No one said aloud the thought in all their minds that if the child Hannah was carrying were a male child it, and not Harry, would be the tenth Earl of the Ainsty.

'What we all need is our beds,' came Miss Godwin's comfortingly ordinary voice. Everyone realized at once that they were very tired. In a few short hours it would be a sunny morning and they had passed the night without sleep. Later they might have the strength to face the events of the night. Just now everything was too much. 'A girl in your condition should not sit on the cold floor, Countess,' went on Miss Godwin, talking to Hannah. 'Come, all of you, back to the house. Never mind the mess. Mr Skellow! Laetitia, my dear! Lord Ainsty! My lord, give your wife your arm. Come, my dear.' She bent tenderly over Hannah and helped her to her feet. 'I will put you to bed myself, my lady. Leave your harp.'

Hannah obeyed without a word, rising, abandoning what was left of her harp and leaning on Miss Godwin's shoulder. Miss Martha took her other arm and together they went down the Temple steps and moved out of sight down the slope.

Godfrey Skellow and Peregrine Akeham followed them.

Harry went over to Laetitia and, putting out both his hands, took her by the shoulders.

'My love,' he said softly. Behind her the embers went out in the tripod on top of the altar of the Oracle of Delphi. 'Laetitia, are you all right?'

'I'm not sure what's been happening.'

'We came up to play out the rites of Apollo, do you remember that?'

'Miss Clare played her harp. I remember thinking how beautiful the music was. Then she began to declaim some verse . . .'

They were alone in the Temple. Harry took her hand in his and once more she did not resist him. He fought against his own immense weariness. It was like a crushing weight, but he must look after Laetitia. As if it were not enough to have married her, in her eyes, under false pretences, they now had to face the fact that he might not have deceived her at all. In the morning, thought Harry. Let her sleep – let us both sleep – and then we can consider what to do.

How could he ever have thought he loved Hannah?

Laetitia came with him obediently. They stood for a while on the top step, with the littered Temple behind them, looking out over the scene.

'How beautiful it is,' sighed Laetitia, then shivered.

'Wait.' Harry went back and found her cloak, dropped where she had first been standing. He wrapped it round her tenderly and they began to walk back to Ramillies.

'I'm so tired.' Her voice was childlike and confiding.

'I know you are, my love.' His own feet were stumbling with weariness. He put his arm round her shoulders and tried to support her steps. His eyes began to close. He blinked, opened them, and every variation of tree and park was printed on his memory.

Ramillies itself. Moon and dawn lit, magical. Long! Would this walking ever end? How many hundred feet of it, that endless façade? All the windows were shuttered, lidded eyes hiding the thoughts of the house. Is it mine? Whose is it? The sleepy warmth of Laetitia pressed on his shoulder and he half carried her along, and they entered their home from the garden, not knowing if it was really theirs or not, and thinking of little but sleep.

They went up to their rooms. Harry took the flowers from Laetitia's hair. He slid off her shoes and, turning back the covers, helped her to slide into bed. Like a baby she sighed and relaxed, stroking the pillow as she settled her cheek on to it.

Harry drew the covers over her and stepped back. All was quiet. Her lashes rested on her cheeks. He went through into his room and wondered if he could stay awake long enough to take off his clothes.

CHAPTER FOURTEEN

The Way Forward

By midday a subdued and heavy-eyed company began to come downstairs at Ramillies. Most of them had breakfasted in bed.

Harry had experienced, not for the first time, pleasure in the luxury of the household at a time when wretchedness of mind made any pleasure unexpected. The steaming hot water brought up to him by his manservant, the new, well-made clothes, the unobtrusive attention.

He had decided to breakfast downstairs and had found himself alone in the small dining-room, helping himself to boiled eggs and slicing off a quantity of cold ham and wondering how, after the night which had passed, he came to have any appetite at all.

It was an odd sensation to know that when he had just embarked on being the tenth Earl – when he had begun to become used to it and to see the place he might take in society – that it might all be snatched away as quickly as it had been presented to him, if Hannah's child turned out to be a boy. He remembered the oracle's last pronouncement: '. . . the next owner of this ground/Before the flight of the sea eagle will be found.'

He could feel nothing except a longing to know how it would affect Laetitia. It was only now that he realized how much he had grown to love her. Without Ramillies, life would be bearable. Without Laetitia, he feared it would not.

After Harry, the next to be down were the Misses Godwin. The room on the east side of the saloon was the one in general use in the mornings, and there they sat on the very edge of the two hardest chairs in their usual precise way. To look at them no one would have thought that they had spent part of the night in a state bordering on madness. They were ill at ease, and had been a little careless in their dress. Otherwise Apollo had left no traces.

'It has been a delight to stay with you, Lord Ainsty,' said Miss Martha. 'Now we really feel we have trespassed on your hospitality long enough. Our home will be missing us, you know. Janey is a good girl, everything will be in order, but Bobbikins, our pussy cat, will nearly have forgotten us and my sister is afraid her canary might be pining away.'

'I will drive my wife over to see you soon,' offered Harry.

'That will be a treat indeed. Do bring the other Countess too, my lord. The ninth Earl's naughty Countess. I'm afraid she has caused a great deal of confusion, poor dear.'

Harry sent for the carriage and before their departure took them into the kitchen garden and sent them away loaded with all kinds of presents, from sweet peas and grapes to melons and marrows.

'What a strange, romantic story,' said Miss Godwin to Harry at the last moment, leaning from the carriage. 'The poor Countess. I feel so sorry for her.'

Harry's lips set into an unaccustomed hard line, but he answered politely that it was very strange and romantic, and privately did not doubt that the news of Hannah's marriage with the ninth Earl would be all round Malton by evening.

It was a scorching day. The sun's heat was beating on the lawns, then rising back in waves of shimmering air. The two lakes must be warmed to blood heat already. The trees seemed to sigh heavily, hanging their dull leaves.

Laetitia came into the morning room. 'Have the Misses Godwin gone?' Laetitia looked pale. She was very calm. Already that morning she had had an interview on household matters with Mrs Gambol. She was wearing a cool gown of white muslin.

'I gave them your compliments, and said that we would drive over soon,' replied Harry, and had time to say no more before Godfrey Skellow came into the room in a hesitating manner. His usual entrances had been all fussy self-importance, but today there was nothing of that about him.

'Lord Ainsty, I think with your permission I will leave today,' he said immediately. 'A most interesting visit. Yes, most interesting. Duty calls, however.'

'I expect you will want to write up our little experiment last night.'

'I think not. I think not, Lord Ainsty, if you will forgive me. Did we all have a touch of the sun? I incline to think so. Too much wine, too, I think. The events of last night are not at all clear in my memory. It is difficult to recall them at all exactly. The vitrified forts of Scotland will be my next field of enquiry. After a short time at home, I will set off to North Britain.'

'Please put me down as a subscriber to your book when you are ready to publish,' asked Harry.

'Most honoured. Now, if you will excuse me . . .'

Hannah appeared in the doorway.

Harry found that he still thought her beautiful, although she had lost her power to move him. This morning she looked haggard, but there was still the noble carriage, the pile of dark hair, the rich, petulant curve of the lip.

At the sight of her Skellow had given a moan and collapsed into a chair.

Harry felt sorry for her and held a chair, saying – he was not sure how to address her – 'Lady Ainsty –' She made a gesture of impatient dismissal.

'I beg you not to call me so. Nor to wait on me. I am in that miserable state which makes life a burden almost too heavy to be borne!' Yet she advanced into the room and sat down on the chair.

'You will excuse me, my lord,' put in Skellow, who saw the way clear between himself and the door, rising and preparing to bolt from the room like a rabbit. 'Goodbye, my lady,' kissing Laetitia's hand. 'Your servant, sir,' to Peregrine, who had just appeared. 'Madam,' to Hannah; and so out.

'Bridges!' called Harry, following his guest into the great hall. 'See that Mr Skellow has everything he requires to transport him in comfort on the next stage of his journey. Perhaps a carriage to York, Skellow? Every attention, Bridges. I hope, my dear sir, that you will be our guest whenever you are in the vicinity.'

'Oh, certainly . . .'

'The carriage went with the Misses Godwin, m'lord. May I suggest the barouche?'

'Whatever is most suitable for our guest.'

'I will see to it, m'lord.'

* * *

It was a relief to be rid of all those not immediately concerned with the discussion which must now inevitably take place. Laetitia had taken up her embroidery and coloured silks and was sitting in the window with her head bent over the satin. Peregrine was still present, with a book on a small table at his elbow. Harry found his presence irritating. He was struggling with himself to be fair to Peregrine. Hannah had moved on to a sofa, and was sitting with her head on her hand and the air of a tragedy queen in a melodrama.

'What folly did we take part in last night?' she cried. 'It is all of a piece. Since I came to this part of the country I have been surprised into folly.'

'You are a sensible woman, madam. What therefore is the cause of it?'

'It is my sensibility. Would that my sense could conquer it!' Hannah struck at her forehead and Harry reminded himself that expectant mothers' emotions are very near the surface.

'Come, madam,' he said firmly, 'can life be so bad? You are surrounded by people who like and respect you.' A glance across at Laetitia appealed for her to uphold him. 'We now know that you are part of our family. Is this so insupportable?'

For a while none of them said anything, but Laetitia put down her embroidery, came to sit near Hannah, and put out her hand to touch the other girl reassuringly on the shoulder.

'Why did you keep your marriage to my cousin a secret?'

'I am a strange compound,' Hannah struggled out the words, 'of weakness and of resolution. He wooed me and I loved him. I have created my own misery, Lord Ainsty. You know my principles. I am against both marriage and inherited wealth. There must be a great defect in my mind! I could not bring myself to give in to him outside marriage. Yet I would not agree to be his Countess and I insisted on its being kept secret.'

'There was no whisper of it at all.'

'We married privately by licence with only the witnesses present.'

'I was the bondsman and one of the witnesses,' put in Peregrine.

'Then why did not you tell me of it?' Harry sounded furious.

Peregrine shrugged his shoulders. 'What was the point when Joshua was dead? How was I to know that he had left progeny behind him?'

'We were only together for two nights in York,' said Hannah.

'Then I insisted on returning for school on Monday morning. He flung off in a temper and went riding in a madcap way across the country, was killed – you know the rest.'

'Why did you not come forward then? You were his widow. You were entitled to honour and respect and a place at Ramillies – the highest –' Harry could not help thinking that when he had first met her, her loved one had been dead under three weeks. Yet she had smiled at him, and he had seen that bewitching dimple.

'My principles are disinterested, Lord Ainsty.'

'Had he lived, it would have become an intolerable situation,' said Laetitia. 'Sooner or later when children began to come, it would have had to change.'

'The basis of any true relationship must be mutual esteem and not material gain.'

'Did you esteem my cousin?' asked Harry.

For a long time Hannah did not answer. When she did speak it was as though the ice were breaking at last.

'What greater misery is there than to love a person whom one cannot esteem or approve of?'

'You thought badly of him,' put in Peregrine.

Her words tumbled out all in a rush. 'Did anyone think well of him? He was intemperate, venal, rash. He drank too much and ate as though there would be no meal tomorrow. He rode his horses to death and abused his servants. Increasing years were likely to increase his faults, not his virtues . . . Yet I loved him.' And for perhaps the first time, Hannah burst into a torrent of tears, for her husband.

'You have brought disturbance and misery to all of us,' sighed Harry. 'My life was obscure but it was happy until Lawyer Crump arrived with his news. The uprooting and readjustment were disturbing, difficult. Then you and I met and your ideas and theories made me miserable. Now you are the Dowager Countess. What the position is of Laetitia and myself we cannot tell. Don't you see that you have acted without consideration for anyone but yourself?'

'I will go away. You will never see me again.'

'But you are with child.'

'Who would have thought it, after only two nights together? Since I discovered that all my plans have changed. I had been intending to stay on at the school for several years.'

'Madam, are you being deliberately difficult? Don't you see that if your child is a son he is the tenth Earl and not I?'

'I do not believe in the hereditary principle.'

'Nevertheless you cannot escape it. We will summon Crump. He will check that your marriage is legal and valid, though I have not a doubt of it. He will confirm that a legitimate male child of my cousin's takes precedence over me and that you cannot shrug off that inheritance any more than I could.'

'What am I to do?'

Laetitia took her hands. 'You must remain here with us. We will live together for the present. May I call you cousin?'

Hannah smiled weakly in a dispirited sort of way and agreed. It was going to be an uncomfortable time for all of them.

'Another schoolmistress must be hired.' Harry wondered wryly whether he ought to take on the post, while he could still nominate himself.

During the heat of the afternoon the two ladies went to lie down and rest in their rooms, and Peregrine went into the north-east facing library. Harry wrote to Crump and then wondered how to start a discussion with Laetitia.

They dined in near silence. The heat of the day was abating, but it had left them too tired to talk much. Later, Laetitia left the room and Harry followed her, to find her in the Garden Room at the side of the house, putting on her pretty straw hat in preparation for going outside.

'May I come with you?' She nodded an agreement. He thought she looked as pale as on the day when she had come to Ramillies as his wife.

Once outside, they found that the day had given way to a sunlit, dreamy evening with a hazy unreality about the landscape.

They took a path to the west of the house, where there was a pleasant area of trees and bushes. A great cedar grew there, where the peacock and his hens had their roosting place. Harry and Laetitia had by now spent so much time in one another's company that they could exchange casual talk, those little fragments of speech which are not planned but escape from the lips, it seems, of themselves. He warned her of an unevenness in the path. She pointed out a new growth of fern. They both remarked on the unusual song of a bird and on the heat of the day, without feeling that they were taking part in conversation.

Then they walked round the park until they came to the little bridge. If they crossed it, they could complete a circuit to the house. The real talk between them could not be put off much longer.

'Were we all taken by some kind of frenzy last night?' asked Laetitia.

'It seems we were. What do you remember?'

'Very little after the fire was lit and Miss Clare began to play on her harp. The music must have been very bewitching. I seemed to go into a dream or trance. Perhaps it was with staying up so late, though I had not felt sleepy as we walked up to the Temple.'

'Do you remember Skellow speaking in a strange great voice? A feeling of devotion? Of dedication, of worship?'

'I remember nothing else.'

'The words that were spoken have changed all our destinies.'

They were standing side by side on the bridge, resting their hands on the parapet.

'How could she!' Laetitia shuddered and Harry knew that she was thinking of Joshua, ninth Earl, and laughed.

'You did dislike him mightily!'

'Very mightily,' said she, recovering her spirits, and with even a hint of roguishness.

'And she is with child. If a daughter, my position and yours remain unchanged. If a son, then he will be the tenth Earl and I will once again be nobody.' Earnestness had taken over. 'I cannot tell you what a grief it is to me to think that I may have so wronged you.'

'Wronged me?'

'By marrying you and later turning out to have no position in society. It is beneath contempt.'

Laetitia, after a swift glance at his face, turned her head away.

'My only consolation is that we are not man and wife in the flesh. You should be able to get the marriage annulled. I could go back to being a schoolmaster. You could find a more suitable match. All would be as it was before. Ramillies and . . . you . . . would be but a dream.'

Had she imagined it, or did his voice falter, almost break, at that point? Did he really care for her? Would he miss her if they parted, as she – oh, how she would miss him! If he loved her, if he were true, what would she not endure for his sake!

'Someone helped me to bed last night,' she said inconsequentially. 'Do you know who it was?'

'It was I,' he said in a voice harsh with emotion, looking away from her and tapping the parapet with his fingers.

'I think, my lord, that you have forgotten that when we were married I then believed you to be a nobody.'

'I know. You blamed me, rightly! Yet I had no intention to deceive. At the time when I asked you, all thought of rank and position was far from my mind. I only thought that we could be happy together.'

'. . . Am I right in thinking that you turned to me after being refused by Miss Clare?'

He groaned. 'Yes.'

'If our marriage were annulled, could you not then marry her? During the minority of the child, assuming it to be a son, you would be ruler of Ramillies and husband of the wife you really wanted.'

There were many answers Harry could have made to this. They crowded into his brain. That Ramillies in itself, with all its loveliness, was not an object – that the position of regent did not appeal to him – that he had lost all desire to marry Hannah –

He turned towards Laetitia, leaned sideways against the bridge, almost unconscious of his movements. Then, as though each word were torn from his body: 'If I am not married to you I will never be married to anyone.'

Their eyes met. They were as still as though they were willow-pattern lovers, painted figures on the pretty bridge. She dropped her eyes, turned, and began to walk past him towards the grass on the other side. He walked beside her. They walked for a while slowly and gently across the expanse of green.

'Let us suppose,' said Laetitia at last, 'that the child *is* a boy. You would not be penniless.'

'Quite penniless.'

'Ah, no. For we had no marriage settlements, in our hasty wedding. Therefore all I was possessed of is now yours. It is I who own nothing. You have many acres, sir, of upland, wild and windy. You have cliffs, grazed by sheep, fronting the cold North Sea. You have tenants; poor farmers, scratching a living from their inhospitable soil. You even have a home; a crazy ruin, miles from anywhere, on whose battlements the raven rests.'

'You should know me better! You might think better of me than that! At the end of our marriage all that was once yours is still yours.'

'And if the marriage does not end?'

'Does not?' Bitterly. 'Can you wait to be rid of me?'

They had lingered across the open space until they had reached a statue near the edge of a clump of trees and both paused. A China rose had taken root here and thrown its branches round the plinth, up to the feet of the statue itself. Laetitia broke off a bloom and, turning to Harry, held it out to him.

'A token of our marriage,' she said.

He put his larger hand round hers, cradling both hand and flower. 'You have not gathered it without pain,' and from her finger he dislodged a thorn, then with great gentleness leaned forward over the rose and kissed her on the lips.

Forgetting all else, they walked on through the park.

Much later, he was to murmur, 'Do you belong to me?'

'Yes . . .'

'Every bit of you?' Touching her bright hair.

'Yes . . .'

'Utterly?'

'. . . Yes . . .'

CHAPTER FIFTEEN

THE OSPREY

The drama of Queen Caroline's return, her rejection by her husband George the Fourth, the country's support for her and her spouse's attempts to discredit her, were soon to come to a dreadful climax.

George had brought in a Bill of Pains and Penalties. The whole assembled Lords of England were to hear the evidence for the Queen and against her. Evidence of her misbehaviour in half-a-dozen of the countries of Europe was to be dragged out in open court, and the newspapers would have the opportunity to revel in publishing all the salacious substance of every servant's betrayal of her mistress. Neighbours she had trusted would retail gossip. Courtiers would reveal the secrets of the back-stairs. Whether what they said was true or untrue, mud would stick and Caroline's name would be damned for ever.

Throughout the country the peers were summoned to attend the hearings and Harry, as the tenth Earl of the Ainsty, among the rest.

'How can I go?' he asked Lord Langbar.

'You will have to go. No one is excused except the very elderly and those abroad who cannot return in time.'

'It may well turn out that I am not the Earl at all.'

'If you aren't, who is? They can hardly summon an unborn child, sex unknown,' and Lord Langbar's eyes were lit with humour.

'The whole business is most distasteful,' went on Harry.

'Which business do you mean? That of the Queen, or your most unfortunate contretemps here at Ramillies? By the way, I think you have been extraordinarily lucky to coincide with the public absorption in the royal dispute. Otherwise your discreet little column in the *Times* and the *York Courant*, to the effect that the ninth Earl had after all been married and there was to be a posthumous child, could have created quite a scandal. As it is, a few raised eyebrows and some months of suspense for you and Letty are likely to be the only result – unless of course it is a boy, which God forbid.'

'It was the forthcoming trial of the Queen that I was actually thinking of. What can it be called but a trial? One is reminded of the worst excesses of Henry the Eighth; and of the trial of Anne Bulleyn. Or of the later trial of Mary Queen of Scots.'

'Those affairs were tragedy. This is nearer to farce. George does not want to cut off her head. He only wants never to see her again. One cannot altogether blame him.'

'I thought you were strong in her support!'

'So I was. Most people were. And I'm not denying that he's a degenerate monster. But she's an unsavoury sort of woman, Ainsty. She could have acknowledged herself defeated and he would have pensioned her off to live quietly somewhere. But oh no. She has to go on fighting and drag out the dirty washing.'

'Doesn't it strike you that that speaks of innocence?'

'Or revenge.'

'Well, I still find it nearer to tragedy than farce. Tragedy for the actors in it and for the nation. We are split from top to bottom; those hot in defence of the Queen and those who fear public disruption.'

'I am glad that Lady Langbar has decided to stay at home. London sounds like an armed camp with all those parties of the military quartered in every village within fifteen miles. Town itself will be full of soldiers. Laetitia is not thinking of coming, is she?'

'Yes. We will both be glad to be away from Ramillies for a while, until things are settled one way or another. After the trial we might go travelling on the continent.'

'There will be no free time in London for junketings. We will be all day at the hearing, listening to a good many sordid details.'

'Neither Laetitia nor I will mind spending our free time quietly together. I have asked my mother and her cousin to join us if they can, and make up a family party.'

'No doubt you will put up with my company from time to time?' asked Lord Langbar gruffly.

'You know that we will both welcome it,' and Harry took the other man's hand in a warm clasp. 'Why not travel down with us?'

The trial was to begin on the fifteenth of August and Harry and Laetitia were to leave Ramillies in the charge of Hannah, Dowager Countess of the Ainsty, and of Peregrine Akeham. Mrs Gambol did not care for this arrangement at all, and it was only her devotion to Laetitia which made her prepared to put up with it. On the whole, Hannah's interesting condition had made most of the female staff soften towards her, but the housekeeper was unbending.

Harry had discovered, on being in the same house as Hannah, that she was very trying to live with. Now that her rigid self-discipline had been shattered and the minor ills of pregnancy were troubling her, she was finding it difficult not to give way to long-repressed moods, to sudden tears and to rebellions against fate.

'I rather think,' said Peregrine to Harry on the last evening before the departure to the metropolis, 'that while you are away I will try to persuade the Dowager Countess to marry me.' Harry looked at him in astonishment.

'I thought your only delights now were arcane knowledge and the black arts, cousin? Did you not connive at some kind of witchcraft, when we spent the night in the Temple of Fortune? Have you still retained any interest in the pleasures of the flesh?'

'What you say may be true. But it is difficult to resist a challenge.'

'You expect to succeed? I did not.'

'But, coz, you are just, fair and considerate. You had no chance of success.'

'Are those qualities so lacking in attraction?'

'Not to your lady wife. But a woman like Hannah Clare needs a rough-shod lord, against whom she can rail, rebel and yet love wildly. Or else one who – like myself – she despises and dislikes, and yet is drawn to against her will. You were no mate for her, my lord. You are now married to the perfect complement in life, for yourself.'

It was true, and Harry felt it more with every day that passed. Laetitia and he were perfect companions, companions for life. They were also finding a love so sweet that they were becoming besotted, each with the perfections of the other. He could have written a sonnet to the least of her eyelashes.

The long trial dragged its length at Westminster until at last the Bill of Pains and Penalties was abandoned. The last shred of reputation left to George and Caroline had been torn away. The country despised him for bringing the Bill and her for behaving in the way which apparently she had. There was little left in life for her, and few enough months to enjoy it in. At the last she showed nobility; having kept copious diaries all her life, Caroline of Brunswick-Wolfenbüttel's last act was to see them destroyed.

The peers were released from their odious duty. Lord Langbar accompanied the Earl and the Countess of the Ainsty on their journey home. The continental travel was put off, for Laetitia was expecting. They were home in time for Christmas.

Hannah's baby was due in March, and when that month came, with promise of spring, it was born and proved to be a baby daughter, which she called Niobe.

The osprey, flying north over the country, passed the town of Malton where Hannah and her infant daughter were paying the Misses Godwin a visit. He was searching for the resting place which, year after year, he found in his journey in the spring of the year. It was sighted; the broad expanse of the north lake at Ramillies.

He dropped down over the domes and spiky outline of the roofs, flying over the bedroom where Harry and Laetitia were admiring their sleeping new-born son, and quietly on his great wings made his stately descent to the water in search of rest and fish.

Only Peregrine, leaning against the shutters of the library window with an ancient volume in his hand, looked up and saw him. Then for a while he remembered a summer night in the Temple of Fortune, and a prophesy about a sea eagle.